# DARK MOON RISING

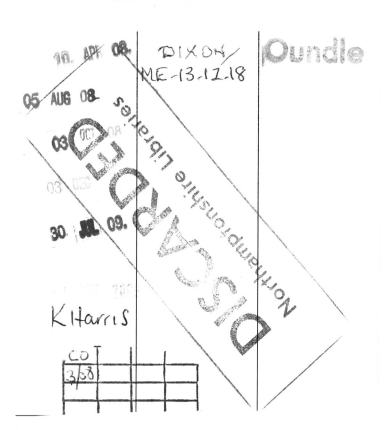

# DARK MOON RISING

Dana James

CHIVERS

**British Library Cataloguing in Publication Data available**

This Large Print edition published by BBC Audiobooks Ltd, Bath, 2008.
Published by arrangement with the Author .

U.K. Hardcover ISBN 978 1 405 64314 6
U.K. Softcover ISBN 978 1 405 64315 3

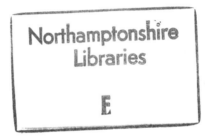
Printed and bound in Great Britain by
Antony Rowe Ltd., Chippenham, Wiltshire

# ACKNOWLEDGEMENTS

I would like to extend my very grateful thanks to: Dr Andy Green and Nigel Halliday of the Geothermal Energy Project; Dr Russ Evans of the Global Seismology Research Group; Ian Main, Dept. of Geology, Reading University; and Jerry Grayson of Castle Air Helicopter Charters. Without their generosity in giving of their time and knowledge, this book could not have been written.

# CHAPTER ONE

Flexing her slim shoulders to ease the strain of concentration, Gena pressed down gently on the lever controlling the Jet Ranger's height. The sun was low in the western sky. Despite the mellow, orange-gold light, it held no warmth. Long purple shadows cloaked the eastern slopes of snow-capped hills and darkened the valleys, and a gusting wind buffeted the helicopter.

Ahead of her and below was her destination. The city stood, grey and forbidding in the dying spring sunshine, on an ochre-coloured plateau. How bleak it looked.

Gena shivered, suddenly aware of overwhelming loneliness.

She caught herself at once. Tired and hungry she might be, but that was no excuse for allowing her emotions to run riot. Pressing the radio transmit button on the stick, she gave her call-sign and requested permission to land.

While the rotors idled and the engine went through its two-minute cooling-down period, Gena wrote up the two logs, one personal, the other a technical record of the helicopter's performance. Over three thousand miles in two days without so much as a loose nut or a leaking valve. It was a real tribute to Jamie's thoroughness.

She was vaguely aware of a muffled figure approaching, but ignored it, anxious to complete her notes. A light tap on the window forced her to look up. Jamie's face, cracked in a huge grin, peered at her through the plexiglass.

She stared blankly at him for a moment, unable to believe her eyes. Then, tugging off headset and safety harness and tossing the log-books on to the passenger seat, she opened the door and tumbled out into his surprised arms.

'Oh, Jamie, I'm so *glad* to see you.'

'I never get a welcome like this from the other pilots.' Jamie's eyes twinkled in his prematurely furrowed face and the gusting wind ruffled his greying hair.

'I can just imagine your reaction if you did,' Gena retorted, drawing shyly away from his steadying hands, angry with herself for allowing the relief and pleasure at the sight of a trusted friend to breach her carefully constructed façade of cool competence.

He grinned in wry acknowledgement, and turned up the collar of his sheepskin jacket. 'Everything OK with the chopper? You haven't had any problems, have you?'

Gena shook her head. 'Not a thing. She goes like a bird, Jamie, smooth as silk. And I pushed her pretty hard on this last leg. I got held up on the refuelling. If those blasted officials examined my papers once, they must have checked them half a dozen times.

2

Honestly, they were crawling out of the woodwork.'

'Come on, Gena, surely you're used to that by now. How many female pilots—*young, pretty* female pilots—do you suppose the Turkish airport staff see in the course of a year?'

Gena made an impatient gesture. 'That's all very well, but with all the delays I could see myself having to spend the night somewhere out in the wilds, miles from civilisation. Anyway, what are you doing up here?' She rubbed her arms. The air was bitterly cold after the snug warmth of the helicopter and the wind had an edge like a scalpel. Despite the Viyella shirt and cable-knit sweater she wore beneath her black flying suit, her name and the company logo embroidered in gold above her breast pocket, Gena began to shiver. 'I thought you were going directly to the base at Van, and I would meet you there after I'd picked up Dr Halman.'

'That's what I thought, too,' Jamie grimaced. 'But the Turkish baggage handlers are about as efficient as British ones. My case of tools and spares was put on the wrong plane, and I had to come up here and fill in endless forms to claim them back. It's OK,' he added quickly, 'it's all sorted out now, and I'm booked on the first flight in the morning.'

'I wish I could offer to take you down with us,' Gena said, 'but I'll have a full load with Dr Halman and all his equipment.'

3

'Don't worry about it.' Jamie grinned. 'I'll abandon myself to the care of a Turkish air hostess. I've heard they're a *delight.*' Gena groaned. 'Mind you,' Jamie sighed, 'what do you bet, now we're so close to the Russian border, I get one that looks like a commissar, complete with jackboots and moustache?'

'My heart bleeds for you,' Gena retorted, grinning.

'Yes, I can see it does.' Jamie patted her shoulder. 'Come on, you're turning blue. Get your things together. We can get a taxi at the gate.'

Following normal company practice, Jamie had booked into the hotel nearest the airport, where Gena's room was already reserved.

While Jamie paid off the taxi, Gena signed the hotel register. The clerk was clearly anxious to leave, glancing frequently at his watch. He beckoned a porter with an impatient snapping of fingers.

'Are there any messages for me?' Gena asked. It was pure reflex. Company policy dictated she inform clients of a phone number at which she could be reached in the event of any change in arrangements.

She told herself she wasn't *expecting* to hear from her father. After all, he had never bothered in all the months she had been ferrying business executives from one European capital to another. But she had never been given a contract like this before.

Nor could several weeks in the eastern highlands of Turkey be compared to a hop from London to Paris or Geneva.

Even getting this job had been a major breakthrough. Ken, Roy and Joe were all on lucrative contracts with a film company, an advertising agency, and a business consortium involved in a takeover. There had been no one else on whom her father could call. Unless he had sub-contracted to another company.

A wry smile twisted Gena's soft mouth. Pigs would fly first.

She picked up her bag and the fireproof wallet containing all her flight documents. For goodness' sake, she chided herself, almost twenty-five years old and you're *still* hoping your father will make a spontaneous gesture of love and approval? Haven't you learned yet that hope only breeds disappointment? She turned away from the desk.

'Just one,' the clerk said. Gena froze. Joy welled up inside her and she felt a strange fluttering in her chest. She whirled round. 'Yes?'

'Dr Halman send his apologies,' the clerk intoned, reading from a piece of paper, his accent thick and heavy. 'He is delayed, but will contact as soon as he arrive.'

'Oh. Thank you,' Gena said quietly. She didn't ask if there were any more. There wouldn't be. She was only getting what she had asked for—no, demanded: to be treated exactly the same as the men.

She looked round at Jamie, hauling her face into a bright smile. 'I'm starving. Give me half an hour to bath and change, and I'll treat you to dinner. There's a restaurant next door.'

Jamie's face fell into worried creases. 'I've already had a look at the menu. I don't recognise *anything*.'

'It will probably be delicious,' Gena assured him. 'I know they eat a lot of lamb and mutton out here.'

Jamie shook his head doubtfully as the porter, carrying Gena's large travel-bag, led them towards the lift.

'So, what's he like, then, this mad scientist?' Jamie asked as they clanked upwards in the iron cage.

Gena shrugged. 'I haven't the faintest idea.'

'Didn't the boss tell you anything about him?'

Gena's smile was grim. 'My father doesn't *know* anything about him, except that he's a geophysicist, a *senior* geophysicist actually, doing research into earthquakes.'

Mouth tightening, Jamie shook his head again.

'You know my father,' Gena tried to make light of it. 'Between squeezing the most out of the Turkish government and worrying about the million-and-a-half-pound helicopter he's entrusting to me, he didn't have much time left for minor details.'

'Hell's teeth,' Jamie exploded softly. 'The man could be a drugs freak, or a groper, or belong to one of these extremist groups . . . *anything.*'

'Gosh, you really know how to boost a girl's confidence,' Gena retorted drily. 'Do you think that hadn't crossed *my* mind?' She drew in a deep breath. 'No, I'm determined to look on the bright side. Using what few facts I *do* have, I've formed my own picture of Dr David Halman.'

'Oh, yeah?' Jamie enquired. 'OK, let's hear it.'

'Well, with that name he's bound to be British, so no language problem. His rank must put him in his mid to late fifties. What else? Ah, yes. His white hair will be all bushy because he hasn't remembered to get it cut. He'll wear his bifocals on a thong around his neck so he doesn't lose them.'

'What about his clothes?' Jamie demanded, entering into the spirit.

'A hairy tweed jacket, with leather elbow patches,' Gena answered at once. 'And baggy flannels. A sludge-coloured woollen shirt, a knitted tie in bilious yellow, and clumpy leather shoes. He'll carry a very large, very old leather briefcase, the kind with a flap and two buckles, bulging with papers. And he'll suck peppermints, for his nervous indigestion,' she finished triumphantly. 'Have I forgotten anything?'

7

'His disposition?' Jamie suggested.

'A real poppet,' Gena announced firmly, trying to convince them both.

Jamie sighed. 'For your sake, I hope you're right.' But his tone was doubtful.

The lift stopped with a jerk and they followed the porter along the corridor.

'By the way, how's Helen?' Gena asked. 'I intended dropping in before I left, but I've had a cold and a sore throat, so it didn't seem wise.'

'I only wish others were as thoughtful,' Jamie grunted. 'Helen's sister came a month ago. She'd had a mild chest infection, and she was still coughing.'

'Oh, no.' Gena frowned.

'Oh, yes. Naturally Helen caught it. Things were dicey for a few days. We're always afraid of pneumonia setting in.'

'Jamie, I *am* sorry. She's all right now?'

He shot her a sidelong glance. 'Do you think I'd be here if she wasn't?'

Gena made an apologetic face. 'Daft question.'

But the added strain had deepened the lines around Jamie's eyes. 'I'm glad you have come,' Gena said softly, 'for both our sakes. I'm going to *need* the occasional glimpse of a friendly face. Perhaps we can have a meal together when I bring the helicopter up for servicing. And the rest and change will do you good.'

Jamie rubbed a hand across his face in a

gesture that betrayed strain. 'You know, even now I still feel guilty about leaving her.'

'Forget it.' Gena was sharp. 'That's the very last thing Helen would want.'

She was the only person at Brady Air Charter who Jamie talked to about his wife's condition. With the others, polite enquiries were met with equally polite but brief responses.

Married for fifteen years, Helen and Jamie had enjoyed the special closeness often found in childless couples.

Two weeks after Helen's car skidded on black ice and smashed into a tree, the doctors told Jamie that his wife would never regain the use of her limbs.

He had stumbled blindly from the hospital, colliding with Gena and almost knocking her over as she came up the steps with a huge bouquet for Helen.

Acting purely on instinct as Jamie's grief pierced her self-protective shell, Gena had thrust the flowers into the arms of a startled nurse, and driven Jamie back to her flat. There she poured glass after glass of brandy into him, and let him talk.

At two the following morning he had passed out on her sofa, still sober despite the alcohol, but totally exhausted, and drained of the incoherent rage that had threatened his own mental stability.

Covering him with a blanket, Gena had

crept away to her own room and lain awake for a long time.

Love? Who wanted it? Love was pain. It meant laying your heart down for fate to trample on. Love was a child offering a clumsily made gift, only for hours of concentrated effort to be met with a cursory glance and an impatient sigh. Love was terrible rows and even more terrible silences as the two most important people in your life tore each other apart. Love was craving approval never to be won because you were the wrong person. Love was wild parties, too much champagne, and one painful, careless coupling in a desperate search for affection. Never again. Love was for fools.

Then she recalled Jamie's pledge to salvage a future for Helen and himself from the wreckage of all their hopes and plans. *Or was love only for the brave?* She had shied away from the thought. Flying was her life, her love. She needed nothing more.

'Gena?' Jamie's voice broke into her thoughts. She looked up quickly. 'Are you all right?'

'Fine.' She nodded brightly. 'I was just wondering how long Dr Halman is going to be delayed. It could be *days.*'

The porter opened the door and stood aside for her to enter.

'Just a minute.' Jamie turned to the porter, speaking slowly and distinctly. 'Does everything

10

work?'

'Is very nice room.' The porter nodded, smiling.

'Yes, but do the lights and the toilet work?'

'Very good. Very clean,' the porter said.

Gena bit the inside of her lip to smother a grin, and raised her eyebrows at Jamie as the porter moved to take her bag into the room.

'Hang on, sunshine.' Jamie laid a restraining hand on the Turk's sleeve. Reaching up, he pressed the light switch and a yellow glow filled the room.

'So far, so good,' Gena murmured, and followed him inside. Jamie disappeared into the bathroom. She looked around.

The room was spartan but clean, with crisp white sheets on the twin beds and brightly patterned rugs on the floor. She heard the toilet flush and a quick rush of water from the shower.

'Why do I get the feeling you're suspicious?' she said as he emerged.

He grinned. 'My light didn't work, nor did the loo. You're not doing too badly. The bath plug is missing, and you may not have noticed yet but those shutters don't close and there are no curtains at the windows.'

Gena shrugged. 'Well, three storeys up, I don't suppose it matters too much.'

Jamie held out his hand for the key. The porter was oddly reluctant to give it to him. Inserting it in the lock of the open door, Jamie turned it several times in both directions. Nothing happened.

'Is very nice room,' the porter said hurriedly. 'Is lovely view.'

'No doubt.' Gena smiled sweetly at him. 'But I don't intend to be one of the sights.' She walked determinedly to the doorway. 'I'm sure you have another equally nice room? With a door that locks? And a plug for the bath?' She glanced over her shoulder at Jamie. 'Don't say it. Where would I be without you?'

It was almost eight o'clock. Refreshed by a long, hot soak, Gena put the finishing touches to a light make-up. The apricot tone of her lipstick added warmth and colour to her creamy complexion. Golden-brown shadow on her lids emphasised her clear grey-blue eyes. Her cropped cinnamon curls had been brushed into a feathery cap that exposed her small ears and curved softly on her neck.

Standing back, she cast a critical eye over the outfit chosen from the very limited wardrobe her weight allowance had permitted. The full-sleeved silky blouse in kingfisher-blue, and black wool jersey skirt which fell in deep folds to her ankles, made a welcome change from the cords, shirts and sweaters she wore every day beneath her flying-suit.

The black patent leather high heels made her feel quite elegant, and she smiled at her reflection. It was nice to indulge her femininity sometimes. Such opportunities were rare. She was going to make the most of this evening.

She could relax with Jamie. Theirs was, in many ways, an odd friendship, but it worked. He had always admired her determination to be a pilot, and had proffered wads of Kleenex and sound advice when her rage and frustration at all the obstacles had spilled over in tears.

She was the only person in whom he would confide his fears for his wife, or the pressures that got to him, knowing she would see them for what they were. He once told her that what he appreciated most was her ability to listen and *not* offer advice.

Once, after she had bumped into him in the lobby of a Geneva hotel with an attractive woman on his arm, he had come to her room and begun a stumbling explanation. But she had cut him off in mid-sentence.

'It's not my business, Jamie. Neither I, nor anyone else, is owed any explanation about your personal life, or how you and Helen are coping with . . . changed circumstances.'

She had watched his face change. As he realised that she understood, his relief and gratitude had been palpable. 'You are looking,' she had said, 'at a leading disciple of the three wise monkeys.' And, though he had smiled, his eyes had been suspiciously bright.

A knock on the door, followed by Jamie's voice, roused her as he asked through the panels if she was ready.

'Almost,' she called back. 'Come on in. I won't be a minute.'

'Not bad,' he allowed, surveying her outfit. 'It's a pleasure to see you looking like a pretty girl for a change.'

'Gosh, thanks,' Gena retorted sardonically, but he continued as though she had not spoken.

'You could do with putting on a few pounds, though, you're all eyes and cheekbones. I know you're as tough as old boots, but to an outsider you could appear . . . decidedly fragile.'

Gena glared at him in the mirror, blusher palette in one hand, brush in the other. 'Has anyone ever told you what a real talent you have for compliments?' she demanded tartly.

He shrugged, spreading his hands. 'I tell it the way I see it. You wouldn't want me to lie, would you?'

'Yes.' Gena nodded firmly. 'I'd be delighted for you to tell me how healthy and athletic I look, like tempered steel, strong and supple and bursting with stamina.'

He snorted. 'You're kidding. A good breeze would blow you away.' But his tone and his expression grew serious. 'Gena—'

'Oh-oh,' she cut in, 'I sense a lecture approaching.' She leaned towards the mirror, wielding the brush with a hand that had begun, very slightly, to shake.

'Gena, listen to me.' Jamie's voice was quiet and held a note she had not heard before.

14

Straightening, she turned to face him, drawing her hands up in front of her in an unconsciously protective movement, brush and palette forgotten. 'I'm all right,' she blurted. 'You said yourself I'm a lot tougher than I look, and I don't need to be the size of a barn to fly a helicopter.'

He shook his head. 'You're only half alive.'

Her laugh was high-pitched, nervous. 'What rubbish! Things have never been so good for me. This job—'

'Is great,' he agreed. 'And no one deserves it more. But it's not enough, Gena. No job is ever enough. People need other people, relationships, love.'

'Not me,' she said at once, her chin tilted defiantly.

'Even you.' His voice was gentle.

'Let it go, Jamie. I don't want to discuss it.' She could hear her own desperation. Retreating into her shell, she turned back to the mirror, cool and brittle. 'I'm perfectly happy alone. Just because *you* can't manage ' Her face whitened and she spun round, appalled. 'Oh Jamie, I'm sorry. I shouldn't have said that. I didn't mean—'

'I know,' he comforted. 'But you're right. Though I love Helen and I'll never leave her, there are times when—' he shrugged helplessly '—it's simply not enough. One of these days you'll wake up, Gena. You'll learn the truth, that you were never born to be one of nature's

15

solitary souls. Inside that prickly shell is a vital, loving woman. I envy the man who discovers the key. He'll have won a rare treasure.'

Stunned, speechless, Gena stared at him. The silence stretched.

Then, deliberately, Jamie turned away, rubbing his hands together briskly, defusing the almost visible tension. 'Right, time to brave the delights of Turkish cuisine, I think.'

Blinking back sudden tears she did not understand—*Jamie believed she was worth loving*—Gena busied herself at the dressing-table, pushing hanky, lipstick and comb into a small black bag.

'Got your Alka-Seltzer?' she quipped shakily.

A sharp tattoo on the door made her jump. Jamie shot her a questioning glance. She shook her head and shrugged.

She started forward, but Jamie stayed her with a raised hand.

'Let me,' he advised. 'It won't do any harm to let whoever it is to know you have friends here. A woman on her own—'

'Oh, Jamie, you do fuss,' Gena chided. 'How do you suppose I manage when you're not around? I expect it's just one of the hotel staff.' She brushed a tiny bit of fluff from her skirt as Jamie opened the door.

'Mr Brady? Gene Brady?'

The deep, resonant voice brought the fine hair on the back of Gena's neck erect.

16

'Er—no,' Jamie replied.

'Forgive me,' the voice, smooth and dark like molasses, was faintly accented and held a hint of puzzlement. 'The night clerk told me Mr Brady was in 304.'

'Well, he got it half right,' Jamie said.

'I don't understand.'

'You will,' Jamie promised, an odd note in his voice.

Darting an uncertain glance at him, Gena started towards the door. Jamie opened it wide and stepped back, gesturing for the newcomer to enter.

Big was the only word to describe him. Well over six feet tall, he was powerfully built with heavily muscled shoulders that even the immaculate tailoring of his dark suit could not disguise.

His hair, black as midnight, was cut short and brushed back neatly from a side parting. Brown eyes set deep beneath black brows regarded her with cool interest. The high cheekbones, strong, straight nose and chiselled jaw resembled rock rather than flesh and bone. Only his mouth, wide and sensual, lips tilted upward in a half-smile of polite enquiry, suggested another, more humane side.

The impact of his physical presence profoundly shook Gena. The room seemed somehow smaller. And she felt . . . *threatened.*

For heaven's sake, she admonished herself, snap out of it. Goodness knew, she'd faced

17

enough government officials in the past two days. And, as all her papers were in perfect order, what possible threat could this one pose?

'This,' Jamie announced, introducing Gena, 'is *Miss* Brady, Miss Ge*na* Brady.'

The upward tilt of the stranger's mouth levelled out. His brows came together to form a straight black bar, and Gena sensed a rapid reassessment taking place behind the expressionless features. 'I see.' He looked at Jamie. 'Then who are you?'

'The name is Drew, Jamie Drew. I'm an aeronautical engineer with Brady Air Charter.'

'And a close friend,' Gena added impulsively.

The stranger shook his head slightly, and Gena decided it was time *she* had a few answers.

'So, are we permitted to know who *you* are?'

The full force of his deep, dark gaze as the stranger turned towards her caused Gena to swallow nervously. She saw his eyes flicker, realised he had noticed the reflexive movement, and lifted her chin. 'What exactly do you want?' Unease, feathering like cold breath down her spine, gave her voice an edge.

The stranger inclined his head. 'Please excuse me. This has come as something of a surprise. I assumed—no matter.' He moved towards Gena, offering his hand. 'My name is David Halman.'

18

Gena's eyes widened. Warm and strong, his hand enveloped hers, but she was barely aware of it. *'You?'* she croaked. 'But—'

The comforting picture she had so painstakingly built up in her mind splintered into a million fragments.

'Is something wrong?' he enquired.

Momentarily bereft of words, she shook her head.

He released her hand. 'I must confess, I did not expect a female pilot.'

Gena stiffened. *Here we go again.* 'Let me assure you, Dr Halman,' her tone crackled with frost, 'I am fully qualified and perfectly competent.'

'I do not doubt it,' he replied, equally cool. 'You would not be here otherwise. My point is that, with so much equipment to deploy at various sites, a man would have been more useful.'

'The contract specified flying, Dr Halman, not labouring,' Gena responded tartly. 'However, should you need help, you have only to ask.'

'How gracious of you, Miss Brady. I'll keep it in mind.'

Behind David Halman and out of his line of vision, Jamie blew on his fingers as though they had just been burned. His quizzical expression brought a quick flush to Gena's cheeks. Her heart was already pounding as a result of the exchange.

19

'Now we have broken the ice,' David Halman said with unmistakable irony. 'I hope you will permit me to take you both to dinner.'

Gena didn't want to go, but a refusal would only provoke questions for which she had no answers. From a professional point of view, eating together made good sense. It would give them an opportunity to discuss the project and their separate responsibilities.

But the undercurrent of tension between David Halman and herself was going to be difficult to ignore. Gena squared her shoulders. What was one more chauvinist pig? She had coped with more than her fair share of those since getting her commercial licence eighteen months ago. At least this one was reasonably polite, despite a disconcerting air of quiet mockery.

'How kind,' she cooed with acid sweetness.

'Look, I'm sure you don't need me—' Jamie began, but got no further as Gena cut in quickly.

'Of course we do.' Her sharpness bordered on desperation. Realisation of what the coming weeks held in store was just beginning to sink in. *Why couldn't David Halman have been the way she'd imagined?* She needed time to adjust, and the reassurance of Jamie's comforting presence. 'The success of the whole project depends on the Jet Ranger's performance,' she babbled. 'I'm sure Dr Halman would agree. We have to make

20

adequate provision for servicing and . . . and
. . . everything,' she faltered, blushing
furiously.

'Indeed,' David Halman agreed gravely.

Startled, suspicious, Gena glanced at him,
and glimpsed a strange light in his dark eyes.

He opened the door. 'Shall we go?'

Gena picked up her bag from the dressing-
table. As she passed Jamie, he murmured, so
softly only she could hear, 'A real poppet, eh?'

Glaring at him, her face on fire, she
marched, head high, beneath the thoughtful
gaze of David Halman and out into the
corridor.

## CHAPTER TWO

Despite a raw chill in the air, the early-
morning sun was warm on Gena's face as she
watched the plane carrying Jamie climb into
the rainwashed sky and head south.

His parting words still echoed in her ears.
After saying he would see her soon he had
added, almost as an afterthought, 'I wonder if
I'll recognise you?'

Puzzled, Gena had glanced down at her
flying-suit. 'Well, I hadn't planned on changing
into scarlet satin and a blonde wig.'

He shook his head. 'That's not what I
meant.' A lop-sided smile twisted his mouth. 'I

knew this would happen one day. Funny the way things work out. I'm happy for you, really I am. But I'll miss you, kid.'

Puzzlement turned to alarm. 'Jamie, what are you talking about? I don't understand.'

He patted her shoulder. 'You will.' His grip tightened momentarily and his voice was slightly hoarse. 'Spread your wings, Gena. You're ready to fly.'

*'Jamie—'*

But he had gone, hurrying up the steps and into the aircraft, leaving her staring after him, bewildered. She shivered with sudden apprehension. Her mind went back to the previous evening.

David Halman had been an attentive host. His conversation had been lively and interesting, and Jamie's attention had clearly been captured by David's brief account of Turkey's vivid and turbulent history.

She, however, could remember little about either the food or what was said. It had been impossible to concentrate with her nerves wire-taut at the prospect of spending the coming weeks with a man so totally unlike the one she had anticipated.

Though he had not appeared to notice anything amiss, Gena had been aware of David Halman's periodic speculative gaze, and had felt herself shrink inside.

She had excused herself immediately after the meal, pleading tiredness and an early start, and had left the two men with their coffee.

'Good morning, Miss Brady. I trust you slept well?'

She jumped. She had not heard him approach. Rich and dark, that voice had haunted her restless dreams. Unable to stem the rush of colour to her face, trying to convince herself it was due entirely to the crisp coldness of the May morning, Gena swung round.

She had never thought she would one day be grateful to all the men, starting with her father, whose patronising derision had taught her so long ago to keep her feelings tightly hidden. But the hard-learned lesson had been infinitely worth while. For, despite the turbulence his nearness and those piercing eyes aroused in her, no hint of it was audible in her cool, calm reply.

'Good morning, Dr Halman. I had a marvellous night, thank you.' Her fingers, hidden in the pocket of her flying-jacket, were tightly crossed. She had to tilt her head back to meet his gaze. One dark brow lifted fractionally, as if mocking the lie. Her colour deepening, she added briskly, 'Are you ready to begin loading?'

He nodded. His black hair, still showing comb marks, tumbled across his forehead, stirred by the breeze. His jaw was freshly shaved and the elusive fragrance of an expensive cologne tantalised her nostrils. It was musky and spicy, and Gena had to fight an overwhelming urge to inhale deeply and fill her lungs with the scent.

Beneath the scuffed leather jacket lined with sheepskin, he wore a cream roll-necked sweater. Olive-green cords were tucked into heavy lumberjack boots which bore the scars of previous expeditions.

It was the boots that reminded her once again of her original image of him. Goose-pimples rose on her skin. How *could* she have been so wrong?

Instead of a suitcase he was carrying a large, double-handled travelling-bag. The briefcase he held in his other hand was relatively new, black, slim, the type used by executives and businessmen. *She hadn't got one single detail right.*

Gena's own flying-jacket, also fleece-lined, was of black leather. Beneath her flying-suit she was wearing blue cords, a blue paisley shirt and her apricot sweater. Fleece-lined black boots over fine wool socks ensured her feet would remain warm, and her coppery hair glinted like a newly minted coin.

'Allow me.'

'I can manage,' she responded automatically, her tone sharper than she intended.

'No doubt,' he agreed impatiently. 'But don't you have more important things to do?' He glanced meaningfully at his watch.

'Especially if we are to reach Ahslan base by lunchtime.'

Gena's head flew up. 'What do you mean, reach Ahslan base by lunchtime? We're going to Van.'

He shook his head. 'There has been a change of plan.'

'Since when?'

'Since last night. Your engineer agreed it was not strictly necessary for the aircraft to undergo a service again so soon. You have done at most only twenty hours since the last one. That is less than half the permitted flying time. And you did tell him, did you not, that the helicopter was flying, *"like a bird, as smooth as silk"?'*

Damn him, he was right. He was the sort of man who would *always* be right. So much for her hoped-for breathing space. She was being catapulted in head-first.

'So it was decided that you and I will go directly to Ahslan and set up the network. Once that is done you will still have time in hand to return to Van for the service.'

There was nothing she could say against the plan. Gena gritted her teeth. 'As you wish.'

'Now that's settled, where would you like our personal luggage?'

Several hundred miles apart, was the answer that sprang immediately to mind, but she thrust it aside. 'On the floor in front of the passenger seats,' she replied, her fingers tightening on the large, silver-coloured wallet that contained all her flight documents. 'That will leave the seats themselves free for anything you can't get into the cargo space.' She was about to add a warning about distributing the weight evenly, but he forestalled her.

'Don't worry about the loading,' he said over his shoulder. 'I've done it before.' You would have, she thought viciously. 'It was a small plane, not a helicopter, but the principle is the same, isn't it.' He was making a statement, not asking a question.

'Then I'll leave you to it,' she said sweetly. She needed a few precious moments alone. This new development needed adjusting to, and confusion about her own feelings was making her head ache.

He nodded. 'The sooner we get on our way, the better.'

Gena walked swiftly, blindly, across the concrete to the airport building. She wasn't dreaming. This was real. It was happening *now*. In a few minutes, with that imperious man beside her, she would be taking off literally into the unknown. David Halman would be with her all day, every day. She would be working more closely with him than on any other assignment. But there was no end-date, no time-limit to cling to for comfort. Nor was there any way out, unless she broke her contract. If she did that, her flying career would be finished, her father would make quite sure of that.

It wasn't the job itself that bothered her, though it was undoubtedly a challenge. She adored flying, regardless of the conditions. The greater the difficulties with weather or terrain, the faster her adrenalin ran, and the more she learned, honing her technique and reactions to razor-sharpness.

No, it wasn't the job. It was *him*. She had met hundreds of men in the course of her work. Many had been highly influential in terms of money and position. Quite a few had been good-looking. Several had been intellectually brilliant.

But she had never met one like him, who apparently combined all those attributes.

A man whose sheer physical impact could shake her to the core, whose arrogance was balanced by an undercurrent of self-mockery that denied conceit, and whose impatience reflected total commitment to his work. That, at least, was something she could understand.

Out of the blue, Jamie's words came back to her. 'I always knew this would happen one day . . . spread your wings, Gena, you're ready to fly.'

Her steps faltered as comprehension dawned. No. It was ridiculous, impossible. Jamie was wrong. She wasn't ready. She never would be. Not for a man like David Halman.

Squaring her shoulders, Gena pushed open

27

the office door.

Forty minutes later, her patience stretched to breaking point, she swept the documents spread out across the counter-top into an untidy pile and began pushing them back into the fireproof wallet.

'I not finished yet.' The uniformed official frowned, clearly surprised by Gena's sudden and decisive action.

'Oh, yes, you are,' she responded tartly. 'You have examined everything but my teeth. We both know my papers are in perfect order. I have filed my flight plan. I've got the weather report, and now I want clearance to leave.'

'Why so much hurry? You not like our city?' The official raised his shoulders, spreading his hands as if Gena's attitude and behaviour were incomprehensible.

'It's a wonderful city,' Gena smiled through gritted teeth. 'But I have a schedule to keep to and you really are making it rather difficult for me.'

'I?' Limpid brown eyes opened wide in astonishment. 'Dear miss, I want only to make pleasure for you. First, I will buy you a delicious lunch. I know special place, very quiet, very clean. The food is—'

'I don't want lunch!' Gena shouted, biting her lip as several heads turned. It took her no more than an instant to read their expressions. Those who were not speculating as to whether the official would get his way were openly hostile. She swallowed hard. 'Thank you all the same,' she added, her voice rigidly controlled, her smile fixed. 'But what I want most is the clearance. I really would appreciate that.'

'What's the problem?' David's deep voice jerked her head round. To her chagrin, a great wave of relief washed over her. She fought it furiously. She didn't need him. She didn't need anyone.

'There's no problem. Everything's fine,' she said quickly, determined he should not think her incapable of coping with such minor inconveniences as an awkward airport official.

'Then what's taking you so long? I finished loading twenty minutes ago.'

Helplessly, Gena shrugged. 'For reasons best known to himself, Ghengis Khan here won't stamp the blasted form.'

David's eyes narrowed, but his tone was polite as he addressed the official in Turkish.

Swelling with self-importance, the man shuffled papers on his desk, indicating Gena with a jerk of his head. Then in a coarse whisper he added a remark in a leery man-to-man tone, and winked.

Gena's sharp intake of breath made a small hissing sound for, though she did not understand the words, their implication was all too clear.

Outraged, she started forward, but David clamped one steely arm around her, pinning her arms to her sides and effectively rooting

29

her to the spot as he bent his head towards the official.

After such a long time any man's arm around her would have felt strange. But to have *this* man holding her, a virtual prisoner, such was his effortless strength, was a shock that sent her every nerve quivering with a distracting mixture of fear and delight.

His soft, scathing torrent of words had the same effect as a machine-gun.

Widening eyes darted from David to herself and back again as the man flinched, then wilted, all colour visibly draining from his face.

Gena watched in awed amazement. What on earth had David Halman said?

Scrabbling for the permit, the official hastily stamped it, pushed it towards David, and backed away with such haste that he almost knocked over his chair.

David's features were a mask of cold contempt. Releasing Gena, he picked up the flimsy paper and thrust it into her hand. 'Come on.' Brusquely he pushed her towards the door. 'Too much time has been wasted already.'

Gena had always prided herself on her ability to ignore provocative remarks and, under normal circumstances, would have bitten her tongue. It was the push that did it. That and the intense frustration of having him march blithely in and sort out the whole unpleasant situation in five seconds flat. *What*

30

*a fool he must think her.*

She shook her arm free of his grasp and quickened her pace, anxious to get ahead of him. 'Perhaps if the men in this country concentrated more on their jobs and less on trying to seduce every female they meet, there wouldn't *be* so much time wasted.'

Effortlessly he caught up with her and she flushed under his quizzical gaze. 'Why did you use that word?'

'What?' Thrown off balance, she looked up at him. 'What word?'

'You said "female", every female they meet.'

'So?'

'Why did you not say "woman"?'

Suddenly wary, Gena shrugged, elaborately casual. 'What difference does it make?'

'A lot, I think.' His gaze was intent. 'Do you not think of yourself as a woman?'

'Oh, for heaven's sake!' Gena erupted in exasperation. 'I think of myself as a *pilot.* The fact that I am a woman has been—*is*—more of a liability than an asset.'

'I see.'

No, you don't, she thought, but did not say it aloud. During the lengthening pause, Gena had an unpleasant suspicion that she had told him far more than she realised or intended. She gave herself a mental shake. She was over-reacting. What she had told him was the truth.

'Then surely you must be used to situations like that?' He gestured back at the airport

31

building.

'Are you trying to justify that man's behaviour?' she demanded.

'No,' he was perfectly calm, 'merely explain it. Though that should not be necessary.'

He was right, that was the infuriating thing. She *was* a woman in a man's world. Of course she would excite comment and reaction. It was up to her to learn how to handle it. Her father's attitude had warned her. He had never shown the slightest sympathy. 'If you can't stand the heat, get out of the kitchen,' had been his only response the first time she had complained of harassment. She had not made the mistake of mentioning her difficulties again.

'I find it extremely irritating when my job is made twice as difficult by other people's inability to move with the times,' she retorted.

'As, in your particular circumstances, that is always going to be an occupational hazard, you either have to accept it, or get out and do something else. It would appear, as you are here, that you have decided to accept it.' He was growing impatient. 'I am not interested,' he added firmly, cutting her off as she opened her mouth to reply, 'in your hurt pride. My immediate concern, and your job, is to get us both to the research site as soon as possible.'

Lengthening his stride, he walked briskly towards the helicopter, leaving her with no choice but to follow, cheeks aflame, stomach

32

knotted with fury at the implication that she, and not that horrible little official, was responsible for the delay.

*Men!* she exploded silently. They were all chauvinist pigs. But her turn would come. Just let him wait. When they hit the turbulence over the mountains it would be interesting to see how arrogant he looked with his face in a sick-bag!

Drawing in a deep breath, her good humour gradually reasserting itself, Gena cast a thoughtful look at the towering banks of cloud building up in the east, and hurried across the remaining stretch of oil-stained concrete.

Just as she reached the Jet Ranger she was aware of a strange sensation in her legs. They felt decidedly weak and trembly. The feeling lasted only a few seconds, but was thoroughly unnerving. She put out a hand, blindly seeking support, and clutched at the cargo door-handle.

About to climb into the passenger seat, David caught the movement. 'Is something the matter?'

'No,' Gena shook her head, 'it's nothing. I thought—just for a minute—' She shook her head again. 'I'm fine.'

Comprehension lightened his features and his mouth quirked. 'Did you feel the tremor?'

'Is that what it was?' She blew a sigh of relief and grinned. 'I thought my legs were going.' Then the significance of what he'd said sank in. 'That was an earth tremor?'

He nodded. 'They happen several times a day. Mostly they're so mild that you don't feel them at all.' He climbed into the helicopter.

Gena stared after him. It was the first earth tremor she had ever experienced, and it hadn't been pleasant. Still, if he could be so offhand about it, there couldn't be much to worry about. On the other hand . . . Gena shook her head. This whole situation was assuming a terrifying resemblance to a runaway train.

She opened the cargo door. One quick glance told her his claim had been no idle boast. She could not have stacked the cases better herself.

After a quick visual check of the outside of the air-craft, she opened the pilot's door, tucked the silver wallet into the pocket within easy reach, then slipped out of her bulky jacket and tossed it on top of the baggage. Climbing into her seat, she shut the door.

David Halman, also jacketless, was settled in the passenger seat, safety harness and lap-strap already fastened.

Gena tried to swallow the sudden constriction in her throat. The cockpit, which before had always been comfortably spacious, seemed unexpectedly suffocatingly small. It wasn't that he was deliberately crowding her. The pilot's seat was entirely separate from that of the front passenger.

Concentrate, she told herself fiercely.

34

Ignore him and *concentrate.*

Struggling into her harness, she fastened it quickly, her fingers becoming steadier, more sure, as she went through the familiar pattern of pre-flight activity.

Reaching behind her left shoulder, she took down the headset with its attached microphone, plugged the jack into its socket on the overhead instrument panel and fitted the set comfortably over her ears.

David Halman laid his hand briefly on her thigh. Light and fleeting though the touch was, it made her start, and she had to force a smile of polite enquiry.

'Do you have a spare set?' His voice and expression were equally polite. But the mockery dancing at the back of his dark eyes told her that her reaction had been noted.

She pointed behind him. 'Put the switch on intercom,' she directed and continued her instrument check, acutely aware of his powerful body, one long, muscular thigh barely inches from hers. He smelled of soap and fresh air and that subtle, musky aftershave.

*Concentrate.* Gena switched on the electrical power and all the gauges jumped into life, needles flickering.

With her left hand she pressed the starter button on the lever that ran between the two seats, then gradually twisted the top of the lever, opening the throttle. As the engine started to wind up, and the rotors began slowly to spin, Gena sensed David Halman's eyes on her.

'Miss Brady?' His voice came through the headset, deep and clear.

Gena kept her eyes on the gauges. 'Yes, Dr Halman?'

'Would it cause you difficulty if I asked you to talk through the take-off?'

Gena eyed him swiftly, searching for tell-tale signs. But there were no creases of tension around the dark eyes, no whiteness at the nostrils. The corners of the wide mouth which could look so cold and forbidding, were tilted ever so slightly upwards, and his hands rested, palm-down and perfectly relaxed, on his thighs. She felt a twinge of shame at her disappointment.

'I'm not suffering from nerves, Miss Brady,' he added drily, and Gena felt herself grow uncomfortably warm. Had her thoughts been that obvious? 'As a scientist, I am permanently curious. This is a new experience for me.'

Join the club. Gena managed to restrain the bubble of hysterical laughter that rose to her lips. Aloud she said, 'It's no trouble.' But she kept her eyes firmly on the instruments.

'You're sure it won't distract you?' he pressed.

'That depends on what you want me to talk about,' Gena replied, scanning the surrounding area to make sure no unwary airport employee was straying too close to the

36

spinning blades.

'I can think of a great many things.' His deep voice contained a ripple of amusement, and something more. Something that caused a peculiar lurching in her chest and brought her head round swiftly, involuntarily, to meet his gaze. 'But for the moment,' he added with a laconic smile, 'perhaps we had better concentrate on the take-off procedure.'

'What did you say to that man?' Gena found herself asking.

David Halman lifted one shoulder in a casual shrug. 'I told him you were in Turkey at the government's request, and that you were working for me on a vitally important project which could eventually save many thousands of lives.'

Gena nodded, rather taken back. She hadn't thought of it in quite such heroic terms, yet basically, she supposed, it was the truth. Even so, the official's reaction had been remarkably dramatic. 'And that explanation was sufficient to change his attitude and make him give me the clearance?'

David Halman hesitated, then his mouth twitched in the barest suggestion of a smile. 'Not exactly.'

'Well? What did, then?' Gena demanded, having a job to curb her impatience.

Dark eyes held hers. 'I also told him you were my woman,' he said calmly. 'And that in insulting you he had insulted me. For that I was sorely tempted to ensure he spent the rest of his unworthy life shovelling sheep droppings with his tongue, a position clearly more suited to his miserable talents than the one he had so grossly abused. But as Allah is merciful, so I would be, *once only.*'

Gena gaped at him, speechless. Of all the patronising, conceited . . . *Arrogant?* That didn't even begin to describe this imperious, egotistical, presumptuous, chauvinistic . . . Then, to her own amazement, and quite against her will, she dissolved into helpless laughter. No wonder the official's self-importance had collapsed like a pricked balloon. *What a threat!*

It was only as he smiled and gave a self-deprecating shrug that she realised how intently he had been watching her, awaiting her reaction.

Gena tried to hang on to her anger. She had every right to be furious. It was absolutely appalling that the official should consider propositioning her perfectly acceptable. But to use the withholding of her clearance as blackmail was utterly despicable. His retreat into grovelling apology only when she was claimed as the property of another, more powerful man reduced her to the status of a mere *thing.* So much for feminism, equal opportunities, and four years of intensive, brain-numbing study followed by constant practice and refining of technique.

'So,' David Halman murmured, 'you do have a sense of humour, Miss Brady. I was beginning to wonder.'

Gena shook her head. 'I don't know why I'm laughing. It isn't funny at all, really. But—'

'Laughter is good for the soul,' he interrupted. 'And when the alternative is tears . . .' He spread his hands, palm up. 'A lecture on women's rights would have been a waste of breath. I spoke to the man in terms he would understand.'

Biting her lip to forestall both another giggle and a shudder at the all too vivid mental image of the punishment with which David had threatened the official, Gena nodded. 'Mmm.'

*You are my woman.* She shivered in earnest and felt her skin tighten. Forget it, she told herself abruptly. He didn't mean it. There's nothing to fear. It had been merely the means to an end. The quickest, most expedient way out of a time-wasting situation.

Clearing her throat, Gena moistened dry lips. 'The engine is presently running at Ground-idle,' she said, her voice gaining strength and confidence now she was back on familiar territory. 'We use the minute or so it takes for the engine to warm up to write up the logs.' She extracted two books from the wallet. 'The technical log contains notes of any minor defects which are non-hazardous and can wait for the next service. The pilot's log records every take-off and landing, the date, time, number of passengers, type of cargo and total weight of the aircraft.'

'How do you work that out?' he enquired as Gena pulled a small calculator from the wallet.

'From the weight of fuel, plus passengers and cargo.' Entering the figures in the appropriate column, Gena added her signature and snapped the log shut. Slotting the wallet back into the pocket on the door she looked across at him. 'All set?'

'You mean we can actually go now?'

This time Gena did bite her tongue. Ignoring him, she snapped on the switches controlling the generator, radio and lights. Winding the engine up to one hundred per cent rotor speed, she pressed the radio transmit button on the stick in her right hand. 'Control, this is G-Brad-One. Request permission for take-off.'

As the affirmation came through the headphones in a crackle of static, with her left hand Gena raised the lever.

'What does that do?' David demanded.

'It tilts the rotors so that they bite the air and lift the helicopter off the ground.' He hadn't been joking when he'd said he was curious. But, unlike some of the passengers she had carried, his interest was genuine and, for the moment at least, centred entirely on the machine.

'What about that?' He indicated the control

40

in Gena's right hand.

'That's the cyclic, commonly known as "the stick". It controls the helicopter's balance in the air. Hovering is actually the most difficult phase of flight. The pilot is operating in three dimensions at once, which requires continual adjustments with stick, lever and both foot pedals. It's a bit like rubbing your stomach and patting your head at the same time. It also requires the most power of any manoeuvre and so is very heavy on fuel. The problem is that whereas a plane *wants* to fly, a helicopter doesn't.'

Gena raised the lever higher and pushed the stick forward. The Jet Ranger rose into the sharp sunlit air and, nose-down, climbed away in forward flight, curving into a sweeping turn to head south.

'And that, as they say, is all there is to it.' She could not keep the mild irony from her voice.

'Quite.' He was watching her every movement. Normally front-seat passengers were more interested in the view. But David Halman was very different from the kind of passenger she usually carried.

'So, why did you do it?' he demanded.

Stiffening, she shot him a sidelong glance. 'I beg your pardon?'

'Why choose this as a career?'

'Why not?' The flippant reply was her stock response.

'That doesn't answer my question,' he said evenly.

'I wasn't aware that answering your questions was obligatory,' she retorted.

'Miss Brady,' impatience edged his tone, 'I was not expecting to work with a woman. You, on the other hand, were fully aware that your passenger would be a man. So why in the name of all that's holy did you accept the job?'

'What do you mean?' Her heart gave an uncomfortable thud as warning bells set up a clamour in her brain.

'Your antagonism.' He was curt. 'Is it directed at me personally, or at men in general?'

'What antagonism?' she parried. 'Just because I choose not to submit to a cross-examination—'

He muttered something violent in Turkish. 'I'm *interested*, that's all.'

'Ah, yes.' She was sarcastic. 'What's a nice girl like me doing in a job like this?' As soon as the words were out she regretted them. Why was she behaving so badly? He had done nothing to deserve it. *He scared her, that was why.* He made her *aware,* provoking thoughts and feelings she didn't know how to deal with.

She swallowed hard. "Forgive me, Dr Halman.' She stared straight ahead. 'I should not have spoken as I did.'

The silence lengthened and she wondered whether he intended to ignore her apology.

42

She tried to convince herself she didn't care one way or the other. But it did matter. It mattered very much. 'I—I love to fly,' she said simply. 'And my father runs an air charter business, so . . .' She shrugged.

'He encouraged you?'

A bitter smile touched her mouth fleetingly. 'Not exactly.'

The memory of her father's reaction when she had confronted him was as vivid now as the day it happened.

It would have been all too easy to settle into the familiar life-style of others of her kind. Jetting to Gstaad or St Moritz for winter skiing, to Rio for the Mardi Gras, to Cannes for the Film Festival. Seeing the same people at the same parties, all looking for new thrills, more excitement, *anything* to lift them out of the boredom of an aimless existence.

She had watched several of her contemporaries slide into the downward spiral of soft then hard drugs. Others had turned to alcohol or promiscuity in a vain attempt to fill the emptiness or blot it out.

The morning after that dreadful night she had crept, bruised and shaking, past the snoring bodies sprawled on the furniture or entwined on the carpet, past the empty bottles and stale food, out into the cold grey dawn.

Scalding tears of rage and self-loathing had streamed down her pale cheeks as she drove through the deserted streets to the place she called home.

If anyone heard her skid to a halt on the granite chippings that covered the drive, they ignored it, used to her arrivals and departures at all hours.

Up in her room she tore off her clothes, rolling the expensive silk underwear and filmy dress into a tight ball to be burned later. Standing under the steaming shower, she scrubbed her aching body until her skin was raw. There were no tears now. No man would ever make her cry again.

Dressed in a pair of comfortable old cords and a baggy sweatshirt, Gena carefully replaced her comb on the dressing-table and made a vow to her reflection. Then she went downstairs and found her father at breakfast reading the *Financial Times* over his scrambled eggs.

'May I speak to you for a moment?' Her legs resembled jelly, but her voice and her resolution were rock-steady.

'What is it?' He did not raise his eyes from the paper.

'I want to fly,' she said abruptly.

'Where to this time?' Irritation and indifference mingled.

'That wasn't—what I mean is, I want to join the company. I want to learn to fly helicopters.'

*That* caught his attention. Lowering his paper, her father studied her for a moment, then returned his gaze to the page. 'No.'

It was no more than she expected. Drawing in a deep breath, digging her nails into her palms, Gena lifted her chin. She might not be the son he had so desperately wanted, but she had his blood, his stubbornness.

'You spent a lot of money on my education,' she reminded him. 'You have seen little return for it. Now, I could continue to fritter away my time and your money in a pointless mockery of everything you've built up. Or I can study for my commercial licence and become a useful member of your staff. Surely that makes more sense, in terms of economics alone?'

'Don't patronise me, young woman,' her father warned. But at least he was listening.

She waited, hardly daring to breathe, in an agony of indecision. Should she try to press him and risk turning him against the idea? Or should she remain silent and chance his refusal on the grounds of her lack of enthusiasm?

He turned aside to open the paper out. 'All right, I'll finance your studies. If you fail the exam, that's an end to it. There'll be no second chance.'

'And if I pass?' she gritted.

'Then we'll see.' He turned a page, shaking the paper smooth and refolding it.

'I want your promise of a job,' Gena said doggedly. 'A flying job with Brady Air Charter. No favours, no concessions. I'll be just another pilot.'

This time Ben Brady did not bother to look

up. '*If* you pass.'

'I'll pass,' she had vowed quietly.

Gena looked across at the dark man beside her, her soft mouth twisting. 'His was a more passive reaction.'

'You had to prove you were serious?'

'Something like that.' She didn't want to talk about herself any more. The fact that he was so open and honest about his curiosity did not make it any easier to deal with. Still, if he could ask questions, then so could she. 'What made you decide to go into earthquake research?'

'Are you asking because you really want to know, or simply to divert my attention?' She detected the familiar undertone of mocking amusement.

'Both,' she answered bluntly.

'I think,' he mused, dark eyes glinting, 'we are beginning to understand one another.'


CHAPTER THREE

Gena made no reply. He was free to think what he liked. She tried to ignore the sudden, uncomfortable pounding of her heart and looked down at the snow-topped hills and rock-strewn valleys. A river, swollen with melt-water, tumbled, foaming, through a canyon.

A shepherd boy, wearing a thick, wide-shouldered felt cloak against the icy wind, and carrying a rifle and a long stick, shaded his eyes to watch them fly over. Neither his huge dog nor the sheep took any notice.

'You want to know why I'm here? My mother's parents died in an earthquake in 1960.' His brief smile faded. 'I was only a child at the time, but I remember my mother's grief. I think it was then,' he turned his head to look directly at her, 'that my career chose me. You see, I had only just begun to know them. There had been some opposition to the marriage between my mother and father. Because although my mother was born here in Turkey, her parents were English.'

'*English?*' Gena gasped, glancing at him, wide-eyed.

'You sound surprised,' he observed, his tone full of irony.

'Yes—that is—no—' She stopped and began again. 'I had *expected* you to be English. But then, when I actually met you, you weren't anything like—' She stopped abruptly, hot colour rising like a tide up her throat to flood her face. She was floundering further and further out of her depth.

'Please,' his voice was silky, 'you must tell me what you *did* expect. I am fascinated.'

*Why not?* Goaded by impulse and a rare sense of mischief, she described in detail the eccentric old scientist she had envisaged.

She pulled no punches, spared no detail,

and when she had finished she risked a quick peep at him, trying to assess his reaction. He had tested her sense of humour. How was his own?

One black brow rose. His smouldering gaze pierced her carefully expressionless façade. She was caught, held, unable to resist his probing stare as it cut through the protective layers to touch her very soul. For an instant she was terrified.

Something akin to electricity tingled through her, charging every nerve-end with its power, leaving her breathless and exhilarated. Without a word being spoken, her challenge had been met and answered.

He began to laugh, a deep, full-bodied sound that warmed her, lightening her heart and lifting the corners of her mouth in an answering grin. 'Now I understand why you looked so shaken.'

Her grin faltered and she studied the dials. No, you don't, she thought, at least, not the whole reason. And I have no intention of telling you.

'Poor Gena! You do not mind if I call you Gena? I think the time for formality is past. We are now colleagues. Who knows?' His laconic tone gently mocked her. 'We may even become friends.'

'Let's not rush into anything,' she retorted drily, and immediately wished she hadn't. Instinct told her he had seen through the quip

48

to the fear which motivated it. A polite reiteration of 'who knows?' would have been quite sufficient, nicely non-committal without seeming rude.

'Aaah.' He struck his forehead lightly with the heel of his hand. 'I forgot, you English need to take time to decide about such matters.'

'You are half-English yourself,' she pointed out.

'Yes,' he agreed. 'But I am also half-Turk, with the blood of four thousand years of war and conquest hot in my veins.'

Gena glimpsed the laughter in his eyes and quickly averted her gaze, staring out of the windscreen. 'You, Dr Halman,' she managed to keep her voice level despite the chaos within, 'are a rotten tease.'

'Call me David,' he said at once. 'Actually, my father named me *"Davud"*, but for my colleagues in Britain and America "David" is easier.'

'You've worked there?' Gena asked, unable to help herself. Well, it was only polite to show *some* interest.

'I did my Ph.D. at Cambridge,' he replied, 'and I've worked for the Global Seismology Research Group at the British Geological Survey in Edinburgh, and also at the Massachusetts Institute of Technology.'

Gena swallowed. 'You've certainly been around.'

'I prefer to say that I have travelled widely,' he corrected, straight-faced. 'I wouldn't want to give the wrong impression.'

Gena was furious to feel herself blushing. 'That's what I meant, that you've visited other countries,' she said quickly. He didn't give a damn what she thought. His reproof was a deliberate nudge to set her wondering about his personal life. Well, she wasn't about to play his games. He could keep a harem for all she cared. 'Anyway, what is this project that you're working on at the moment?'

'You mean why do I need you and all these instruments out here in the back of beyond?'

'You took the words right out of my mouth.'

'Oh, no.' His irony matched her own. 'You would have phrased it far more politely. But to answer your question,' he went on, not giving her a chance to retaliate, 'I received information from Kandilli Observatory concerning an area which had previously been designated a seismic gap—'

'Excuse me,' Gena interrupted in sugary tones. 'I know I must seem terribly ignorant, but would you mind telling me what a seismic gap is?'

'Forgive me, it is a fault of mine to expect too much of people.'

'Then no doubt you spend a great deal of your life disappointed.'

'No,' he replied thoughtfully. 'Surprised perhaps, philosophical even, but not

50

disappointed. A seismic gap,' he went on, barely pausing for breath, leaving Gena uncertain yet again as to who had come out best, 'is an area along a fault line or within a known earthquake zone where, for reasons we do not yet fully understand, all earth movement stops. To give you a rough idea,' he raised his hands, palms together, sliding one up against the other. 'Pretend my hands are two parts of the earth's crust. A fault line is where they meet and move past one another. But if this movement stops, then pressure begins to build up. The longer the two parts are locked together, the greater the pressure. A good example is the San Francisco end of the San Andreas Fault.'

All thought of scoring points forgotten, Gena looked quickly across at him. 'So what happened to this seismic gap, the one you're interested in?'

'It has suddenly started showing signs of activity,' David told her. 'We've managed to pinpoint the area. 'It's up in the Müsguney mountains. By setting up a network of seismographs—those are instruments which register movement within the earth's crust—I will be able to record the foreshocks and any other warning signs.'

A shiver feathered down Gena's spine. 'Does this renewed movement mean there might be an earthquake?'

'No.' His calm smile made his next words all

the more shocking. 'It means there *will* be an earthquake. I hope to trap it within the array of instruments. The information I obtain will be invaluable in helping discover if there is a pattern, or sequence of events which regularly occurs before a quake.'

Gena moistened dry lips. Had her father *known* what he was sending her into when he told her she was to ferry a scientist and his gear out to a research base? She had been vaguely aware that Turkey was a country where earthquakes sometimes occurred, but no one had bothered to mention the fact that she would be actively involved in searching for one.

'D-do you have any idea how long before . . .?' Her voice tailed off. The enormity of it was too great to absorb all at once.

He shook his head. 'No, which is why I want to get to the base as quickly as possible and get the network set up.' He glanced across at her. 'You're taking all this very calmly.'

'Now you sound surprised,' she accused.

'To be perfectly honest, I am. I don't know many w—people,' he corrected himself quickly, 'apart from other geophysicists, who would accept what I've just told you with such equanimity. We will, after all, be living above the shop, so to speak.'

Gena shrugged. 'Hysterics would not alter the facts.' She threw him a wry grin. 'Just be thankful you can't see what's going on inside

52

my head.'

'If it's any comfort, this project and the information I collect could mean the difference between life and death for millions of people who live in earthquake zones.'

'How?' she queried.

'If there *is* a pattern and we can relate it to a time-scale, it would mean that warning systems linked to evacuation plans could be set up.'

She hadn't thought of that.

David continued, 'Unless the earth actually opens up and swallows someone, which is quite rare, very few people are killed by the quake itself. But the *results* of an earthquake— falling buildings, fire, tidal waves, exposure, and disease due to contaminated water or lack of medical facilities—can kill thousands. If people could be moved out of their homes, offices and factories *before* the event, having obeyed the basic rule of turning off cookers and dousing all fires, much loss of life could be prevented.'

Gena swallowed. 'So it's pretty important, this project.'

He nodded. 'I hope so.'

Immersed in what David was saying, and coming to terms with how it affected her while automatically maintaining their course, Gena had not noticed the heavy blanket of black cloud rolling in to shroud the mountain tops and obscure the sun.

A scatter of hailstones hit the windscreen

with a noise like lead shot, and a sudden gust of wind buffeted the helicopter and sent it slewing sideways.

Adrenalin poured into her veins, sharpening every sense, speeding her reactions. The sky grew dark and the hail smashed into the Jet Ranger's plexiglass and metal shell. The noise was deafening, and it took all Gena's skill to control the aircraft and hold their course. With visibility almost nil, she was flying solely on instruments. The hail turned to a slushy mixture of driving sleet and rain that threatened to clog the wipers. 'Come on, come on,' she murmured as the machinery laboured.

She suddenly remembered her passenger. 'You OK?' she shouted without taking her eyes from the dials and gauges.

'Yes,' came the brief reply.

At least he knew when to keep quiet. Thank heaven he had more sense than to distract her with jokes or unnecessary chatter.

As swiftly as it had arrived, the squall departed. The clouds rolled onwards and the sun re-emerged. Gena blinked at the sudden brightness and let her breath out in a soft rush.

'Does this sort of thing happen often?'

Still on an adrenalin high, her senses super-acute, Gena detected an odd note in his voice.

'How should I know?' She grinned. 'This is your country, your weather. I simply deal with conditions as they happen.' Then it dawned. Quickly she looked across at him, noted his

54

pallor, the tiny beads of sweat on his upper lip.

'There's a bag in the pocket on your door,' she said.

'What?'

'If you feel sick.' Gena wanted to savour the pleasure of revenge. He deserved it, didn't he? He must be feeling rotten. No one could look like that and not be suffering.

'I will not . . . I am fine,' he said firmly. She knew he was trying to convince himself as much as her, and felt reluctant admiration and a strange tug at her heart. Previous experience had taught her that male passengers who got air-sick were more noisy, demanding and badly behaved than any child. Yet he had not uttered a single word of complaint. 'Do you by any chance carry water?' He kept his gaze riveted on the windscreen.

Gena reached into the pocket on her door and drew out a small box with a cellophane-covered straw attached. 'Apple juice,' she said as she handed it over. 'I find it more . . . settling.'

'Thank you.'

She heard him pierce the box and swallow deeply, and masked a smile at his sigh of relief. 'Don't worry about it,' she said softly. 'Everyone gets queasy at some time or another.'

'You didn't,' he pointed out.

'I'm used to it. Besides, it's always easier when you're at the controls. Having something

55

to do takes your mind off how you're feeling. There isn't time to think of both.' She grinned wryly. 'Wait until the earthquake.'

Their eyes met for an instant and the warmth in his made her recoil as, in a knee-jerk reaction, fear gripped her, knotting her stomach and drying her throat. Looking away quickly, she reached for their map and passed it to him, careful to avoid any physical contact. 'Would you mind showing me exactly where the base is?' Her stilted politeness jarred and she sensed puzzlement in his swift glance.

The thick paper crackled as he opened then re-folded it to a manageable size, showing the right area.

Leaning towards her, his shoulder touching hers, his dark head close, he tapped the map with a long index finger. The nail was clean and cut straight across. 'There's Ahslan.' His breath was warm against her cheek.

Her whole body was aware of his nearness, every nerve alive and quivering, partly in fear, but partly from a strange, nervous excitement. Her throat was so tight that she couldn't swallow, and her heart hammered painfully against her ribs. *Please don't let him hear. Don't let him know.*

'You see it?'

'Yes, yes,' she answered, too quickly. 'Thank you.' She altered course slightly, heading south-east.

David turned his head to look down at the

56

foothills and valleys rushing by beneath them. They flew on over occasional pockets of human habitation. Near a stream a few roughly built stone houses huddled together as if for warmth and comfort amid the cold vastness of the barren landscape.

Several kilometres further on, half-way up a gently sloping hillside, the ruins of an ancient city gleamed like bleached bones in the spring sunshine.

'It's so . . . big, so empty,' Gena murmured.

'I think, after your crowded little island, anywhere would seem big and empty,' David teased. 'Soon we should be able to see the highway . . . yes, there it is.'

Gena craned her neck, frowning. 'Where?'

Leaning towards her, he clasped her shoulder with one hand and pointed with the other. *'There.' His* movement was a spontaneous action of impatience.

But Gena, flinching at his touch, her nostrils full of the scent of him, felt her cheeks growing hot.

Desperately, she followed the line of his pointing finger and saw at last the thread of asphalt winding through the hills. 'OK, I've got it.'

'Ahslan is over to the left, roughly between those two peaks, about another forty kilometres.' He released her and settled back. 'It's right up in the mountains and there are no roads. Even the tracks between villages change frequently.'

'Why's that?' She was still acutely aware of him, but had her erratic emotions tightly curbed.

'Landslides,' he replied succinctly.

'But with no roads, how did you get all the buildings and equipment up there? And why choose such an isolated place anyway?'

'For precisely that reason,' he explained. 'No roads, no traffic, no people, means no reflected human sound or vibration to distort the instrument readings. But I cannot take credit for setting up the Ahslan base. It was established several years ago by another team. The army brought everything up by transport helicopter. The building was put together in sections.'

'That was useful—the army, I mean.'

David nodded. 'It is good practice for them, and all the research bases in the area are assured of fuel and food deliveries even when weather conditions mean we are cut off at ground level.'

'So there are other research teams out here?'

The ironic lift of one dark brow told Gena her train of thought was all too obvious. David nodded. 'I think there are three at the moment. One from Bogazici University in Istanbul, one from Cambridge connected with the British Geological Survey and one from the Natural Environment Research Council.'

'How long have they been operating?' Gena guided the Jet Ranger into the mountains, her eyes darting between the jagged, snow-clad peaks high on either side to the compass in front of her and back again. Every minute took her deeper into the wild heart of this unpredictable country and further from everything familiar.

David shrugged. 'Some of the bases are permanently manned, with new teams replacing old ones after a given period to carry on very long-term experiments. Often a team will consist of several specialists in different fields all working on different projects which are inter-related.'

'H-how long, roughly, would their experiments take?' Gena asked, ultra-casual.

'It varies. Some take only a few weeks, others last months or even years.'

'I suppose, with most of you so far from home,' Gena ventured, 'you enjoy getting together to exchange news and results.'

David looked at her. 'I don't think you understand. The bases are spread out all over eastern Turkey. The nearest one is over one hundred kilometres from Ahslan. Sometimes it's a problem even to obtain radio contact. Visits are out of the question.'

'Oh.' Gena swallowed, trying to ignore the horrible sinking feeling in her stomach. She gave a self-deprecating shrug. 'I guess I haven't quite got used to the distances out here yet.' But there was worse to come.

'*There,*' David said suddenly, grabbing her shoulder and pointing. 'Down there. That's Ahslan.' He patted her arm. 'Congratulations, that was a superb piece of navigation.'

His praise went unnoticed as she stared down. They were at the head of a wide, deep valley. From foothills on either side, the mountains soared skyward, their peaks playing hide-and-seek behind swift moving clouds.

Gena swung the helicopter in a wide circle. A small pre-fabricated building painted bright yellow stood on the only piece of level ground in the entire area, just below the summit of a steep, craggy hill, and protected by a huge rocky outcrop. A radio aerial, sprouting antennae like a Christmas tree, stood atop the rocks, held in place by wires and shackles. Thick cables led down from it to the back of the building. There would be just enough room to land the Jet Ranger between the building and the tumbled rocks forming a protective windbreak.

Slowly, she brought the helicopter lower. With nothing to help her judge the wind's speed or direction, she had to rely entirely on the *feel* of the aircraft and her own technical skill. But the warning bells growing ever louder at the back of her mind had nothing to do with the landing.

The skids touched the bare ground as lightly as a falling leaf, and the helicopter settled.

'Well? What do you think?'

She heard the irony in his voice as she looked out at the place which was to be her home for the next few weeks. 'It's . . . very small,' she murmured.

David was already unfastening his safety harness. 'It's spacious compared with some,' he countered brusquely. 'You'll find it has all the essentials. And after all,' he paused and waited for her to look at him, 'we've already established that you want to be accepted on merit alone, no special treatment or privileges. That is right, isn't it?'

She had no choice but to nod. But why weren't there any lights on? Why had no one come out to meet them?

'Come on, then. I'll show you round.' He smiled, his tone droll. 'It won't take long.'

'You go ahead, I have to let the engine cool and write up the log.'

David removed his headset and unplugged the jack. 'Two minutes, then. There's a lot to do.'

'Then you'd better get started. I have my own job to finish before I can help you with yours.' She hadn't meant to sound quite so tart. His brows climbed and an apology trembled on the tip of her tongue, but she bit it back and turned away to extract the wallet.

Perhaps she was wrong. Perhaps the other members of the team were—She bit her lip. Who was she trying to fool? There were no *others.* Ahslan base had been empty until their arrival a few moments ago. She was alone here with David Halman. That was the truth of it, and she had better start getting used to the idea.

Slamming the wallet back into its pocket on the door, Gena climbed out. The icy wind cut through her like a knife. Grabbing her flying-jacket, she quickly pulled it on and turned the collar up around her ears.

The sudden splutter and throb of an engine made her jump. A door slammed and David walked round the corner of the building, dusting his hands.

'What's that?' Gena asked, shivering.

He looked mildly surprised. 'The generator. All our heat, light and cooking facilities run off electricity.'

'What about water?'

'There's a holding tank up in the rocks.' He pointed. 'It's filled from a stream. The water is piped into the cabin to the sink in the kitchen and the shower. We even have a flush toilet, though there's no septic tank. The waste is piped away down the hillside to a crevasse.'

Gena gaped at him. 'There's a shower?'

'What did you expect? A brisk rub-down with a handful of snow? Or perhaps you assumed that in a backward country we would be content to live in squalor?'

His laconic remark cut far too close for comfort and Gena felt her colour rise. 'I—I didn't . . . I meant . . . to be honest, I hadn't thought that far. You caught me by surprise. I was still wondering . . .'

'Yes?' His dark eyes challenged, cool and mocking. He clearly had no intention of making the situation easier for her. So be it. She'd cut her tongue out rather than admit what she had really been thinking. Did he expect her to give him the satisfaction of hearing her admit she hadn't anticipated, *and didn't know how to handle* this much equality? Hell would freeze first.

'I was wondering whether you planned to begin setting up the network this afternoon?' Determinedly, she matched his coolness. 'Of course,' she added pointedly, 'I can't be sure of the weather, or the flying conditions.'

He shrugged, apparently unmoved. 'We'll just have to take a chance on that.' Opening the passenger door, he reached for his own jacket. 'But the answer is yes. I want the stations deployed and recording as soon as possible.'

'Fine,' Gena replied briskly. 'Do you want to eat first? Or shall we just throw our bags inside and go at once?'

'I do admire your enthusiasm,' David remarked drily. 'However, stamina is far more useful in a situation involving hard work, long hours, and,' a brief smile touched his lips as he added softly, 'more than a little tension. So, I suggest we pace ourselves.'

Tight-lipped, her cheeks rose-pink, Gena gave a brief nod. Why was he always *right?*

Hauling a large cardboard box off the back seat, he dumped it into her arms. 'I was told there's a stock of tins in the kitchen cupboard. I've brought fresh fruit and vegetables, bread, yoghurt, cheese and meat. The army will fly in more fresh food, diesel for the generator and fuel for the helicopter at the end of the week. You take the food in, I'll bring our bags. You know,' he murmured, 'under different circumstances, this might have been quite romantic.'

Gena whirled round, a biting retort already forming, and collided with him. 'Oh!' she gasped.

'Go on.' He frowned impatiently. 'Get inside, you look frozen.'

Staggering under the awkward weight, frustrated, angry, convinced her life was rapidly spinning out of her control, Gena tottered up the steps to the open front door.

'The receiver-room is straight ahead, kitchen on your left,' David said behind her and, with an eerie sense of inevitability, Gena crossed the threshold.

David kicked the door shut behind them. Gena shivered. It smelt cold and dank, unlived-in.

'I've turned the thermostat right up,' he said, passing her with their bags.

'What kind of system is it?' Gena asked,

64

gazing around in rising horror.

'Ducted hot air. In an hour the whole place will be comfortably warm.'

'In an hour, we'll be out working,' she objected.

He nodded. 'But just think how nice it will be to come home to.' He opened a door and with an ironic smile disappeared.

Gena picked her way across the grey-marbled floor covering coated with old, dried muddy footprints, and dropped the box on to the draining-board. The sink unit and cooker stood in an alcove. There was a window above the sink and another further along the wall. Both were protected on the outside by a thick metal grille. Beneath the larger window stood a large cupboard and a battered fridge.

Attached to the back wall was a fold-down table and, in front of it, two plastic-topped stools, their grey-painted metal legs chipped and peeling. Left of the table was a closed door. Gena guessed the pair of double doors on the right hand wall led into an airing cupboard.

The remaining space was filled by two easy chairs with grubby fabric covers, and a low oblong table scarred with cigarette burns and ringed with the stains of countless coffee-mugs. The whole room, not counting the alcove, was barely ten feet square.

David re-entered the room empty-handed. Gena was so preoccupied, it did not immediately occur to her to ask what he'd done with the bags. Just his presence made the place seem even smaller.

'You don't call *this* squalor?' The words were out before she could stop them.

His features tightened. 'It's basic,' he agreed. 'But it is a research base, not a hotel. The men who use it work up to eighteen hours a day. As long as they have food and a warm bed within four dry walls, they tend not to worry about the finer points.'

Gena turned to the sink. The stainless steel was dull and streaked with accumulated grease and coffee grounds. A grey rag rested, dry and stiff, over the tap. She pulled a face.

'Of course, if you feel a desperate urge to give the place a woman's touch, you're free to do so,' David said, coming towards her.

'How generous of you,' she murmured acidly.

The alcove in which the sink and cooker stood was barely two and a half feet wide and, as David positioned himself between her and the rest of the room and started taking things out of the box to put them away, she was gripped by a sudden feeling of claustrophobia.

'Just keep in mind that the project comes first.'

'My thoughts exactly,' her reply was crisp. 'I was employed to fly a helicopter, not to play house.'

David turned to her and, though she had to

tilt her head back to meet his dark gaze, she stood her ground.

'Look,' he reasoned, 'to make our stay here even moderately comfortable, we will both have to compromise.'

Gena's mouth was stubborn. 'I'm not cooking.'

'Do you expect *me* to do it?' he demanded impatiently.

'Why not?' she rapped back. 'You eat, don't you?'

'What has that to do with it?'

'Everything. Why should I do all the domestic work? Just because I'm a woman?'

'Could you strip and service the stand-by generator?'

She stared at him.

'Well? Could you?'

'Not *all* of it,' she admitted. 'I know how to clean and reset the spark plugs, change the oil, and clean out the carburettor'

'Our generators are diesel not petrol-driven.'

'Oh.'

'So, could you test the radio links with the outstations and calibrate the signals?'

'No, but . . .'

'Can you move the twenty-gallon fuel drums to make room for the new delivery at the end of the week?'

Gena gritted her teeth. 'You know I can't.'

'Then who is supposed to do all that while I

prepare meals?' She looked down. 'Gena, if you had been a man we would have shared all the jobs outside our own specialities equally.' He pushed one hand through his hair. 'As it is . . .'

Gena swallowed, and clasped her hands in front of her. 'I think there's something you should know.'

'Yes?' He waited.

Gena cleared her throat. 'I can't cook, either.'

In the stunned silence, David's eyes widened, then narrowed as he muttered something brief but fervent in Turkish. 'What sort of woman *are* you?'

It was said more in exasperation than anger, but Gena flinched. 'Not the sort *you're* used to, obviously.'

'You can say that again,' he murmured.

'Well, that's your problem, not mine,' she retorted.

'Didn't your mother teach you anything?' he demanded, clearly bewildered.

Gena caught her breath. The shaft hit deep. 'My mother left home when I was eight years old,' she flung at him. 'I never saw her again. Excuse me,' she muttered and pushed between him and the sink, blinded by sudden tears. She grabbed a jar of coffee from the box.

*Damn him!* she raged inwardly, her throat stiff and aching. He caught her arm. She froze.

'I am so sorry.' His voice was full of

68

compassion, and in that instant she hated him. She didn't need anyone's pity.

'Forget it,' she said flatly. 'Where does the coffee go?'

'In the cupboard.' He pointed. She put the coffee away and took a bottle of olive oil from the box.

It was David who broke the silence. 'Was there no one? No aunt or grandmother to . . .'

Gena clasped the bottle to her, fingering the cap. 'Our housekeeper was not the maternal type, and my father's lady-friends were all too busy with their own concerns to be bothered with an obnoxious child.' The glance she threw at him was candid. 'And I was very obnoxious. It was my revenge on the world. So I was packed off to boarding-school. Several of them, actually. I think two years was the longest I stayed anywhere. Tight-lipped headmistresses would frown over me, heads would shake, then a letter would arrive on my father's desk suggesting I might be happier elsewhere. I coasted through university, and by the time I was twenty-one I was living in the fast lane, foot hard down, heading for disaster.' She stopped, appalled, biting hard on her lip.

*What was she doing?* Something about David Halman seemed to short-circuit her normal caution and reserve. She dragged in a deep, shaky breath.

His questions stirred up memories she

would rather forget, fears she didn't know how to handle, hurt that was almost too much to bear, and a deep, despairing loneliness she had tried so hard to deny.

Grasping her shoulders, David turned her to face him, studying her intently, his expression puzzled. *'You? I* don't recognise the person you describe.'

Gena shrugged, acutely aware of the warm weight of his hands, simultaneously craving and fearing his touch. Edgy, her nerves jumping, she began to tremble.

'What happened? What changed you?'

'That's none of your business,' she flared and, wrenching free, stumbled backwards and pulled open the cupboard door.

'The oil is kept in the wall cupboard above the sink.' David's voice was cold. 'I think it will be quicker if I put everything away. Perhaps you could fill the kettle and make us some coffee?' He was icily polite. 'You can make coffee, I presume?'

Inwardly, Gena winced. She deserved that. 'Yes, I can make coffee. W-would you . . . shall I do sandwiches as well?'

He grunted something unintelligible.

Gena squeezed past him, picked up the kettle, and turned on the tap. The pipe hammered and gurgled, then water shot out, hit the bottom of the sink, and bounced. She gave a startled cry as the shock of icy spray hit her in the face, making her jump back. The

70

kettle slipped from her fingers and clattered into the sink, diverting the flow up the wall. Gena dived forward and turned the tap off again.

In the silence, she blinked and looked down. Drops of water beaded the front of her sweater and trickled down her leather jacket.

She heard a muffled snort behind her and whirled round. David was having great difficulty keeping a straight face.

'I think,' he pronounced, his dark eyes glistening, 'that after a few weeks of living with you, an earthquake is going to seem like light relief.'

Gena wiped her face with the back of her hand, glared up at him, and to her own amazement started to giggle.

## CHAPTER FOUR

But, even as she laughed, hot tears pricked her eyelids. *She was the joke.* Fate seemed to be conspiring to show up her every flaw. She wasn't usually awkward or clumsy, and keeping her emotions under lock and key had been relatively easy, *until yesterday.*

As for cooking, she had never needed to learn. At home Mrs Manning had always done it. At school it had clashed with her physics lesson. At university she had used the cafeteria

71

or the local take-aways. Then, when she had moved into her own flat, she'd been so busy studying, she'd relied on fruit, yoghurt and convenience foods, or ate out.

Keeping her face averted, she moved away from him. Trying to look purposeful, she crossed to the table and set it up, bending double to make sure she really had got the support in the right place. It only needed the damn thing to collapse with all the lunch dishes on it to completely demolish any hope of him treating her as an equal or taking her seriously.

Her back to him, she blinked the tears away. What did it matter what he thought? Professionally he couldn't fault her, and, as that was her sole reason for being here, who cared about the rest? So why, all of a sudden, did she feel so . . . inadequate?

Dragging out the stools, Gena placed them firmly on either side of the table. Conditioning, that was all it was. Because she wasn't expert at a woman's traditional role, she was less of a woman. Never mind her intelligence or her professional accomplishments. They paled into insignificance alongside the shocking fact that she could not cook.

Well, so what? She heard him close the fridge and place the empty box on top of the cupboard in front of the window. He had filled the kettle and it was be-ginning to boil.

'Make the coffee, will you?' he directed. 'I'll see to the food.'

'I said I'd do that,' she protested automatically.

'We are in a hurry,' he reminded her, his tone caustic. 'Don't worry, you'll get your chance. Once the signals start coming in . . .' His brief gesture implied she would have it to do whether she liked it or not.

'How kind.' She smiled at him through clenched teeth.

Twenty minutes later Gena pushed her empty plate aside and poured herself a second cup of coffee.

'Mmm, please.' David nodded as she held the pot up in silent query. 'Have you had enough to eat?'

She grimaced. 'Too much, I think. It was delicious.' Her surprise was met with a sardonic glance as David rested his back against the wall and extended his legs, crossing one booted foot over the other.

'It's simple enough. Goat's cheese with tomato and pepper in pitta bread, with a side-dish of chopped cucumber and onion in garlic-flavoured yoghurt. It's filling, nourishing and takes only minutes to prepare.' His eyes gleamed. 'Slaving over a hot stove never appealed to me either, but as eating is necessary for survival it seemed only sensible to make it a pleasure.'

Rebellion stirred in Gena, but she dipped

her head. 'Point taken.' She raised her coffee-mug, eyeing him over the rim. 'Did *your* mother teach you how to cook?'

He met her gaze. 'Some things, yes. I have three brothers and two sisters. We all had to take our turn with jobs in the kitchen. She was progressive, a believer in equality, at least among children. When my father and mother married, she became a Muslim and adopted Turkish customs. But she remained very English in her belief that boys should not be ignorant of the work involved in running a house.'

'It must have been chaos,' Gena muttered. 'And as for the noise . . .' She shuddered and took a mouthful of coffee. It tasted bitter as she tried to ignore the vivid image of a busy, happy household and the gut-wrenching envy it provoked.

'It was family life.' He shrugged. 'You would like my mother.'

Gena lowered her mug, clasping it in both hands, gazing at the steaming liquid. 'Ah, but would she like me?' There was an unconscious poignancy in her tone.

'She would admire your achievements. But like you? That would not be so easy.'

Gena's head jerked up, immediately defensive. 'Oh?'

'For someone to like *you,*' David said deliberately, 'you must first like yourself.' He drained his mug and set it down.

'Thank you, Professor Freud,' Gena replied sarcastically.

David looked at his watch and stood up. 'Let's go. It's after one, and we lose the sun earlier up here in the mountains.'

'What about the dishes? Wasn't that included in your training?' Despite her disgust at her own pettiness, Gena still could not stop the snide remark.

The look David gave her, a mingling of pity and distaste, made her cringe inside, and she hated him even more, knowing she deserved it.

'It's a matter of priorities,' he said evenly. 'The dishes will still be here long after the daylight has gone.'

She got up quickly. 'I—I just want to . . . which way is the bathroom?'

'Through there.' He indicated the door behind her. 'On the right. The other door leads outside to the fuel store and generator shed. Don't be too long.'

She glared at him, but his level gaze, as hard and black as onyx, warned her against voicing the retort that sprang to her lips.

Her mouth curled in disgust at the grubby towel on the rail alongside the basin. Heaven alone knew how long that had been there.

A toilet, shower cubicle and hand-basin had been crammed into the confined space. There was just room to get from one to the other. Gena closed her eyes as a feeling of suffocation engulfed her, tightening the muscles at the base of her skull. Dewed with perspiration, she drew in a deep breath, forcing herself to relax. She had to look on the bright side. How would she have felt if there *wasn't* a bathroom, if the only facilities were a handful of snow and a hole in the ground?

Heaving a shaky sigh, she grinned wryly. This was luxury. After washing her hands and shaking them dry, she automatically looked round for a mirror, but there wasn't one.

Tidying her hair by touch, she smoothed her sweater down over her hips and went back into the kitchen. Before she had a chance to say a word, David handed her her jacket.

'Go and get the engine warmed up. I'll be with you inside two minutes.'

'Yes, *sir.*' And to think she had felt she owed him an apology.

Seething over this further example of his imperiousness, she snatched her jacket from him and marched out, quite forgetting that she had intended going to her bedroom to comb her hair and repair her lipstick.

But settled in the Jet Ranger, her pre-flight checks complete, Gena's equanimity returned. This was her world, her security. No one could take this away from her. All right, so she couldn't cook. But there was nothing to stop her learning, was there? She was ready for another challenge, and it couldn't be *that* difficult.

She'd never had the time, or the inclination,

before. However, once the out-stations were in place she might be very glad of something to do to keep her mentally and physically occupied. She had brought several books with her, but they certainly wouldn't be enough on their own.

No, learning to cook was a good idea. It had nothing to do with *him*. It was entirely her own decision.

David emerged from the cabin carrying a pick and shovel wrapped in sacking which he laid on the floor behind the front seats.

As he climbed in beside her, fastened his harness, and put on his headset, her restored good humour and new sense of purpose made her smile.

He seemed mildly startled. 'Is something wrong?'

She flashed him a wry glance. 'Because I smiled?'

Slowly the corners of his mouth turned up. 'I have never known a woman like you.'

Gena checked the dials and peered out through the windscreen to gauge the gap between the wall of rock and the spinning rotors. 'I think we've had this conversation before.'

'Why do you assume I am making a criticism?'

'It was last time.' The helicopter lifted off smoothly, backed away from the ledge, and swung round in a wide circle to head down the valley.

'You took it that way. It was not intended as such.' As Gena remained silent he went on, 'I admit your apparent lack of domesticity did surprise me, until you explained about . . . your family circumstances. Now I understand.'

Gena's grip tightened on the stick. She swallowed. 'I was very rude to you. I'm sorry.'

He made a brief gesture with his right hand. 'Please, it is forgotten. Now I think we must concentrate on the job to be done. We will talk again this evening.' It was a statement that left no room for doubt or argument.

Gena turned her head for a moment to meet his dark gaze. Her heart gave an extra thud and she caught her breath. 'If you like.'

Behind her offhand reply, she felt horribly vulnerable and uncertain. Talking with him would be like stirring the bottom of a pool. Who knew what would arise to cloud the water? Yet if they didn't talk, how could she get to know more about him? And she had to admit that she did want to know him better. He intrigued and infuriated her. He put her on edge. He seemed to brush aside all her usual defences and went straight to the heart of her confusion and fear. No man had ever aroused such antagonism, defensiveness—and tentative yearning.

'I'll look forward to it,' he said softly, and the look in his eyes set her heart racing. 'Right.' His tone was suddenly firm and brisk.

78

The subject was closed. 'I want to place the out-stations about ten kilometres apart on alternate sides of the fault.'

She nodded, then looked at him quickly. 'What fault?'

'You see the ridge running along the valley floor?' He pointed.

'Yes.'

'That is the most visible portion of this particular fault line.'

'And that's where the earthquake will happen?' It was so close to the base.

He shook his head. 'Not necessarily. It could be anywhere along the fault, but all the signs say, and I have to admit I'm hoping, it will be within fifty kilometres.'

Not trusting herself to speak, Gena tried to swallow her fear. It left a metallic dryness in her mouth. She was here. She had a job to do. The only escape lay in total concentration.

For the moment the sky overhead was a clear, translucent blue. But in the east, towering clouds formed massed ranks and crept inexorably forward. Inside her warm clothes Gena shivered. Was it an omen?

By six o'clock, the sun had disappeared behind the mountains and cloud blanketed the sky. The temperature hovered just above freezing and the wind, gusty and fitful, hurled flurries of hail and sleet at the Jet Ranger as David slammed the cargo door on the pick and shovel and clambered back into the passenger seat for the third time.

'I think we'll have to call it a day,' Gena told him as he rubbed his hands to restore warmth and circulation. 'The light is going fast.'

'I was going to suggest it,' he agreed. 'We can place the two remaining stations tomorrow.' He gave her a penetrating look as she turned the helicopter round and headed back up the valley. 'Are you all right?'

I'm shattered, she thought, but didn't say it. Instead she admitted only, 'I won't be sorry to get back. Not being able to land at all made it more difficult and more tiring than I expected. It certainly is rough country up here.'

'For what it's worth, I've never flown with a better pilot. And before you ask, I've done a lot of flying in a variety of aircraft.'

Gena usually disdained compliments, relying on self-appraisal for a more critical and accurate assessment. Some of her passengers were so nervous of flying that just getting them to their destination in one piece invested her with the combined qualities of angel and genius.

But this time she could not prevent a delicious glow spreading through her. It took the edge off her exhaustion and filled her with the warm satisfaction of a job well done.

'Some of those cross-winds nearly took me off my feet,' David said. 'Holding the aircraft in a hover while I got the boxes of instruments out must have been a nightmare.'

Gena shrugged, feeling the knots in her shoulders and the tension at the back of her neck. 'All part of the service. Though we have used more fuel than I expected. We've got more than enough to get us back to base,' she added quickly, and grinned at his visible relief. 'You don't fancy a bracing thirty-kilometre walk?'

'I know I specified a need for stamina,' he retorted, his dark eyes gleaming in the reflected light from the instrument panel, 'but I can't recall mentioning masochism or martyrdom.'

'No sense of adventure,' she sighed.

'We'll see about that,' he threatened, and Gena bit the inside of her lip as her blood thrilled to their mutual teasing.

While she wrote up the logs, David disappeared into the cabin. Gena saw warm light spill from the window and her hand fell still.

Dusk filled the valley. In this vast, barren wilderness the cabin was the only source of warmth, comfort and protection. Yet within those four walls lurked a different danger. One which warned, challenged, *beckoned.* Beneath her warm clothes her skin tightened in sudden apprehension.

Switching off the motor, Gena slid the wallet back into its pocket on the door. Then, after a final check that all was as it should be, she climbed out, gasping as the bitter wind

81

took her breath away.

Huddling into her jacket, she hesitated as she reached the cabin, and looked back at the helicopter. It seemed well protected from the gusts, but if the wind backed round to the south . . .

'I think I'd better try and rig up some sort of harness or anchor,' she announced, closing first the outside, then the kitchen door.

She was unaccountably relieved to have something *impersonal* to talk about, a work-related problem to deflect her mind from the intimacy of the situation, and how much David Halman's tall figure seemed to dominate the small room.

His sweater sleeves pushed part-way up his forearms, David stood in front of the draining board, slicing onions on to a plate. A pan of water bubbled on the stove.

'I've got sleeves and stays to stop the rotors whipping.' She took off her jacket and hung it on the hook next to his. 'But I think I'd feel happier if I had something to secure the skids.' Unzipping her flying-suit, she stepped out of it and hung it over her jacket.

'Surely the helicopter is too heavy to tip over?' he suggested. 'And it is tucked well in behind the rocks.'

Gena pushed her hands into the front pockets of her cords. 'You're probably right. It's just . . . well, apart from the fact that my father will hold me personally responsible for every scratch, the Jet Ranger is our only means of getting out of here.'

He gave her a sideways look and scraped the onions into a frying pan. 'Why so anxious to leave? The fun hasn't started yet.'

Gena's heart did a slow somersault. 'I presume you mean the earthquake?' Her tone was light, but she couldn't quite meet his eyes, and her face felt as though it was on fire.

'What else?' His deep voice was so blandly innocent, she knew he was deliberately taunting her. What had possessed her to start this conversation?

'Is there anything I can do?' she asked briskly. 'What are we having?'

'Lamb chops with rice, onions, red peppers and green beans,' he replied. 'I think I can manage the meal.' She winced at his undertone of irony. 'But you might like to make up the beds and put hot-water bottles in. I'll refill the kettle as soon as I've put the rice on. You'll find everything in there.' Still holding the knife, he indicated the double-doored cupboard. 'There should be clean towels as well. If you finish before I do, you could clear the table and reset it.'

The sheets and blankets were warm as she lifted them off the slatted shelves. At least her bed would be comfortable. It would also provide the privacy and solitude she needed. Without that breathing space, she suspected she might find her enforced proximity to

David Halman very hard to handle. She closed the cupboard doors.

'Through there.' He indicated the door alongside the alcove. 'I'm afraid you'll find it rather cramped.' He went on slicing the peppers. 'But as I mentioned earlier, the base is usually staffed by men.'

'Yes,' her smile was acidic, 'I do remember.'

He didn't look up, but continued chopping and slicing, his movements deliberate, relentless. 'And you did say that you were not expecting any special concessions.'

'Don't worry,' she retorted. 'I'm only thankful I don't have to sleep in here.'

His mouth quirked in a brief, almost secret smile. Still he did not look up. 'What a remarkably sensible attitude.'

'As if I had a choice,' she muttered. Hitching the bed-linen up in her arms she marched, chin high, through the doorway he had pointed to—and stopped dead.

The room was scarcely large enough for the two beds that stood at right angles to one another, each jammed against a wall. The only other item of furniture was a chest of drawers.

Frantically, Gena looked around for another door. It was pure reflex. The cabin wasn't big enough for two bedrooms. He had known that. She spun round, her mouth open to protest. And with a strangled groan clamped it shut again.

How could she complain? Especially after,

84

only moments before, agreeing with everything he had said about not wanting special treatment. *But share a bedroom with him?* That was impossible. There had to be an alternative. The kitchen? Hardly, unless she pulled the two easy chairs together and slept sitting up. Then what kind of state would she be in for flying? Conditions up here were particularly demanding. If she wasn't fit to do her job, David would be perfectly entitled to fire her. And if he did that her father would have her out of the company so fast she'd break the sound barrier.

Sucking in a deep breath, she turned slowly back to the beds. There was nowhere else for her to go.

David had put his luggage on the bed nearest the door. Grudgingly, she allowed it made sense. Apart from its being wider, it meant he would be closer to the receiver-room should alarm bells start ringing during the night.

'Can you manage?' Totally devoid of inflection, his deep voice floated through to her, accompanied by the mouth-watering smell of frying onions.

'I have made beds before,' she yelled back, hurling sheets and blankets on to his mattress in her frustration as a feeling of helplessness spilled over.

'Good.' The drawled reply made her madder than ever.

Hauling her bags on to the chest of drawers, she snatched up a blanket and shook it out with a snap and started to make up her bed. Because of the lack of space she could move the foot only a few inches out from the wall, and twice barked her shins on the iron frame as she stretched to tuck the bedclothes under the mattress.

Hot and breathless from her contortions, she picked up the pillowslip, only to realise there were no pillows. Cursing under her breath, she wrenched open the door and marched out to the airing cupboard once more.

'Two for me,' David said. He turned the chops over and slid the pan back under the grill. The aroma of the cooking meat made Gena aware of how hungry she was, hungry, exhausted, hot, sticky and *furious*. 'I like to read in bed. I hope that won't disturb you?'

This apparent consideration for her, when all along he had *known*, was the last straw for Gena.

'Nothing you do in bed could possibly disturb me,' she shot back, and wanted to die as his dark brows rose slowly.

'That sounds remarkably like a challenge,' he observed.

She clutched the pillows as if they were a life-belt, her whole body aflame with embarrassment. 'And that is typical male ego.' It took every ounce of will-power to meet his gleaming gaze. Inside she was a quivering jelly of mortification. 'I also read at night,' she announced in a voice that shook only very slightly, 'and I sleep very well. So please, do not concern yourself on my account.' Head high, drawing the remnants of her dignity about her, she swept into the bedroom, slamming the door. Eyes closed, she leaned against it, her legs trembling uncontrollably, and tried to fight the panic that threatened to overwhelm her.

She didn't even know *why* her heart thudded with such sickening force. She could take care of herself. Slim she might be, but she was also fit and strong. In any case, so far he had treated her with nothing but courtesy, even if his patience had worn thin at times.

His voice through the door made her start, and her eyes flew wide open.

'You're not going to be long, are you? The meal is almost ready.'

'C-coming,' she stammered, and dived forward to finish making the beds. She had got exactly what she'd asked for, total equality. Despite his teasing he was treating her as 'one of the boys'. *No privileges, no concessions.* But now, with a flash of insight that knocked her completely off balance, she recognised that between men and women total equality did not exist.

David and she might be on the same intellectual level, and her endurance might match his. But physically she was weaker, and emotionally far more vulnerable.

This had nothing to do with will-power, or lack of it. For sheer, stubborn determination, Gena knew she would take some beating. The difference was one of nature, of biology, and the gulf was unbridgeable.

The revelation left her paralysed. She had fought so hard and so long for acceptance *as an honorary man.* Today, she had achieved it, only to see her victory for what it was: a sham, empty and worthless.

Her desperation to win her father's approval and to escape the burden of womanhood had led her to challenge men on their terms. She had proved she could fly a helicopter as well as any man. But she could never *be* a man, and she was afraid to be a woman. How many years, how much energy had she wasted chasing a distorted vision?

She sank down on the foot of David's newly made bed. All her anger and irritation with him had been her mind's frantic attempt to deny what was really happening. For the first time in five long years, her emotions were totally beyond her conscious control.

She clasped her head in her hands as realisation washed over her with the shock effect of an icy wave. She was profoundly attracted to David Halman. He stirred feelings in her she had never experienced before. Feelings that disconcerted, enticed, *frightened.*

This awakening of her senses, this new perception of herself was in direct contrast to the way of life she had chosen.

'Come on, Gena.' The bedroom door opened and David leaned in. 'If you haven't finished—' Mild exasperation turned to concern. 'Is something wrong?'

She was already on her feet. 'Of course not.' Busily, she brushed blanket fluff from the front of her sweater, keeping her eyes lowered. 'I was just on my way out.'

'Oh, yes?' His scepticism was all too obvious. 'Then why were you sitting on my bed?'

'I banged my shin,' she retorted, sliding past him, careful to avoid his eyes. 'I did it twice, as a matter of fact, trying to tuck the bedclothes in. I've got a cupboard in my flat that's larger than that room.'

He closed the door and followed her to the table where two steaming plates awaited them. 'Have you done any damage?'

'Iron bedsteads can take a lot of punishment,' she responded tartly.

'Really? I'm delighted to hear it.' His instant reply, delivered in a deliberately ambiguous tone, brought swift, hectic colour to her cheeks. 'But I was referring to your leg. Did you hurt yourself?'

'It's not something I'd want to make a habit of, and my shins will probably resemble a rainbow by the morning, but,' she shrugged, 'apart from that, I'm fine.' She sat down on the stool, noticing how he waited until she had done so before sitting himself. The little courtesy unnerved her still further, though she could not have said why.

'I'm certainly ready for this,' she announced brightly. 'I can't remember when I've felt so hungry.' It was a lie, her stomach had contracted into a small tight knot. 'It smells delicious. I think it always makes a difference if food looks nice as well. The green beans and red peppers add such colour . . .' Her voice tailed off. She was babbling. She had to get a grip on herself.

She caught his gaze. Behind the amusement was curiosity, and something else . . . *respect?* Ducking her head quickly, convinced she was seeing only what she wanted to see, Gena picked up her knife and fork. Would she be able to swallow?

But with the first mouthful her physical need for nourishment overcame her panic. The hot food soothed both her stomach and her frazzled nerves. The room was warm. David seemed absorbed in his own thoughts. Gradually, Gena began to unwind. But, as she did so, her tiredness collapsed on to her like a wall.

David carried their two empty plates to the draining board and returned with a bowl of grapes and a plate of shelled almonds.

Resting her elbows on the table, Gena let

90

her head fall forward and rubbed the back of her neck. She smothered a yawn.

'Someone could do with an early night,' David said quietly.

Gena shot upright, clasping her hands in her lap as panic skittered along her nerves. 'I'm fine,' she insisted. 'Just loosening up a bit, that's all.'

'Looking at you right now,' he said drily, ' "loosened up" is not a phrase that springs immediately to mind.' His features softened. 'But that's hardly surprising. It hasn't been the easiest of days for you.'

Gena attempted a grin and lifted one shoulder in wry humour. 'I've known worse.'

'Even so, I want you to know I admire the way you have accepted all . . . this.' From his hesitation, Gena knew he was including himself as well as the state of the cabin and the sleeping arrangements. 'Nothing was quite what you expected.'

'True,' she admitted, 'but as you say, I'm adjusting. It's all part of the job.' Heaven forgive her for the lie.

'That may be so. But your job is finished . . . for to-night,' he added as her back stiffened. 'I have some work to do in the receiver-room. Why don't you have a hot shower and an early night? You'll probably be fast asleep before I come in.'

She realised he was trying to make things easier for her and, paradoxically, she resented it. Instead of simply thanking him and taking advantage of his offer, Gena found herself protesting. 'There's still all the dishes to do and neither of us has unpacked yet. Anyway, there's nothing wrong with me. It was just pleasant to stop for a few minutes.'

She wasn't going to play the weak, grateful little woman, then have him accuse her of not pulling her weight. She had never been beholden to anyone. She wasn't about to start now. 'You go ahead, do whatever you have to. I'll tidy up here.'

Exasperation drew his brows into a heavy, dark line. 'Has no one ever told you independence can be carried too far?'

'No,' she said flatly. 'I've been told a lot of things, but never that. I am an only child. My father wanted a son and my mother didn't really want a child at all. Being something of an inconvenience to both of them, I learned the value of independence at a very young age. No allowances were made for me then, and I don't expect any now. I'll do my share.'

His eyes narrowed and he studied her for a long, thoughtful moment. Then, saying simply, 'As you wish,' he took a handful of grapes from the bowl.

'Would you like some coffee?' Gena asked with formal politeness. She had meant what she said. He had cooked the meal; the least she could do was make a pot of coffee. A knotted muscle in her shoulder twinged and she rubbed it unthinkingly.

David shook his head. 'Not now, later perhaps. Is your shoulder bothering you? I will not assume it is a sign of weakness if you say yes,' he added, and Gena winced as the barb found its mark.

To her amazement, Gena found herself apologising. 'I—I suppose I have been a bit . . . prickly.' She kept her head bent.

'You remind me of a cactus flower,' he mused, 'delicate and fragrant.' His voice hardened, but beneath the irritation ran a thread of laughter. 'And surrounded by a barrier of thorns designed to keep the world at bay.' The laughter faded and a different note took its place, something she could not identify. 'But though the barrier is a protection, it is also a cage. You would do well to remember that, Gena. Now, turn around.'

She raised her head, suspicion clouding her grey eyes like smoke.

He sighed. 'Gena, have I done anything, anything at all, since we met to harm you?'

Reluctantly she shook her head. 'No.'

'Do you have any reason to believe I *intend* to hurt you in any way?'

Her heart racing, her thoughts chaotic, Gena had to face the truth. He had done nothing. It was *her* awakening, *her* reactions that were causing all the trouble. 'No,' she muttered hoarsely.

'Then you have no reason not to trust me?'

93

The pause was slightly longer, and she had to swallow the dryness in her throat, but in the end the answer had to be the same. 'No.'

'Then do it. Trust me. And turn around. No, remain seated.'

After a moment's hesitation she swivelled on the stool until her back was towards him. 'What are you going to do?' She could hear the apprehension in her voice.

He didn't reply, and she heard the rubber-tipped feet of his stool squeak as he drew closer.

'David?'

'Hush. Just close your eyes.'

She flinched as the warm weight of his hands descended on her shoulders. He let them rest there, unmoving for several seconds.

'Relax, Gena,' he ordered softly. He didn't know what he was asking.

'I—I can't,' she blurted. 'I don't . . . I—I'm not used to being touched.'

After a silence which to Gena seemed endless, he said briskly, 'Then it is time you were,' and, using his thumbs, he began to massage the curve between neck and shoulder.

Her nerves were so taut, her skin so sensitive, that despite the thickness of shirt and sweater she gasped with a mixture of pain and shock. But, as the slow, circular movements started to ease the tension, and the knotted muscles gradually loosened, she groaned aloud with relief. 'Oh, that's marvellous.' The words slipped out of their own volition. *But it was the truth.* Heat seemed to radiate from his hands and flow deep into her tortured muscles, releasing months of accumulated strain. Her head dropped forward and she gave herself up to the wonderful feeling of release.

He worked his hands slowly up her neck, his fingers resting lightly on either side as his thumbs gently kneaded, smoothing away the stiffness and tension. Gena felt as though she was floating, drifting on a warm, tideless sea. Curving his fingers so that his nails lightly scratched her skin, he pushed them up her neck and over her scalp.

With a quick intake of breath, Gena shuddered at the delicious sensation. He repeated the movement a few times more, then, drawing both hands softly down her neck, he rested them for a brief moment on her shoulders. A quick squeeze and they were gone, and vaguely she heard his stool scrape on the floor.

'Ohhh.' She gave a breathless, strangled groan and slowly straightened up, rotating her head and flexing her shoulders. 'I think my bones have melted.'

'For someone who doesn't like being touched—' he began, but she interrupted, correcting him, still slightly dazed and barely aware of what she was saying.

'I said I wasn't *used* to being touched.'

'One is usually a result of the other.'

'Yes,' she admitted softly, then, 'what were you going to say?'

'Nothing . . . It was nothing.'

Gena turned on her stool. She felt . . . *different.* In fact, she couldn't remember the last time she had felt so calm and relaxed and at peace with the world. 'Come on, you can't just stop. Tell me.' She was completely unaware of the transformation in her appearance. She had no idea how vulnerable she looked—or how desirable. Her blue-grey eyes had a luminous glow and her cheeks were softly flushed. 'Please?' Her smile was dreamy, sensuous.

He stood up, an abrupt movement that made her start and sent his stool clattering on to its side. Setting it upright, he glowered at her. 'Such games are dangerous, Gena.'

She stared up at him, her smile fading, uncertainty taking its place. 'I don't understand.'

He studied her with such fierce intensity that she felt hot colour flare beneath the laser-like gaze. 'No,' he murmured at last in a tone that blended wonder and mockery. 'I really believe you don't.' There was a fractional pause, as though he was about to say something but thought better of it. 'I'm going to do some work,' he announced brusquely.

Something had changed. There was a new tension, a silent vibration in the air. Gena was aware of it, but still caught up in her delight at the languorous afterglow of his touch. She sighed deeply and stretched. 'David?' He looked back over his shoulder. 'Thank you for the massage. I—I've never had one before. It's amazing. I feel so different, all sort of . . . warm and pliant.'

His mouth twitched briefly as if in pain, and self-mockery edged his voice. 'My pleasure.'

'Who taught you?' she asked, a mischievous light dancing in her eyes. 'I suppose it was your mother?'

He opened the door, his dark eyes suddenly opaque and unreadable as they met hers. 'No,' he replied starkly. 'My wife.'

## CHAPTER FIVE

Gena stared at the closed door, her body numb, her mind screaming. Part of her clung to self-preservation, already feverishly rationalising, reducing his answer and all its shattering implications to something she could accept and cope with. So he was married. So what? They were working together, that was all. He didn't *mean* anything to her. For heaven's sake, she had only known him a couple of days. What could you possibly feel for someone in that time?

The pressure on her concerning the

contract had wound her up and sent her emotions into overdrive. But it was no big deal. After a good night's sleep she'd have it all under control. Meanwhile, she would keep busy. That was the answer. When she had done all that needed doing, and heaven knew there was plenty, she'd find more. She would make jobs, if necessary.

There simply wouldn't be time to think, *to feel*. But the other part of her, the newly awakened woman, wanted to howl her rage and frustration to the cold, empty hills.

Throwing the grey rag into the pedal bin, she tore an old tea-towel in two and used half to wash the dishes. By the time she had finished scouring the sink and cleaning the cooker with the other half, she was almost dropping with fatigue.

She was just pouring boiling water on to the coffee when David re-entered the kitchen. He hesitated, as if he hadn't expected to see her.

'Why are you still up?' he demanded, his tone surprisingly sharp. 'You look exhausted.'

'Thanks,' she replied shortly. 'I'm just going for my shower. Here's your coffee.' She pushed the mug along the draining board towards him.

'You're not having any?'

She shook her head. 'Goodnight.'

'Gena?' His voice was abrupt, with an underlying note of strain.

She looked up at him. 'Yes?'

He hesitated, his dark eyes brooding. 'Sleep well.'

'You too,' she murmured, and turned away.

Lying between the coarse clean sheets, her feet on a hot-water bottle, Gena gazed out through the curtainless window, through the wide mesh of the metal grille, to a black sky scattered with diamond-bright stars. As her eyelids drooped and closed, she wondered briefly about the grille. Why was it there? She would ask David in the morning. David. *Under different circumstances this might have been quite romantic.* Her eyes filled and she bit her lip hard. She was tired, that was all. It had been a very fraught couple of days.

A tear slid from the corner of each eye, ran down her temple and into her hair. Her sigh caught in her throat, and sleep claimed her.

Gena woke to grey light and the incessant drumming of rain. For a moment she couldn't remember where she was, and reared up, muzzy-headed, on one elbow. Then she saw the other bed, *David's bed.* It was empty, the bedclothes kicked back. The door was shut, and beyond it she could hear him moving about. She glanced at her watch. *Eight forty-five!*

With a horrified gasp she flung back the bedclothes and was about to swing her feet to the floor when, after a brief knock, the door opened and he walked in.

Wearing cords, a check shirt and thick socks

on his shoeless feet, he was freshly shaved and his black hair neatly combed.

Acutely aware of her own dishevelment, Gena grabbed the covers and hauled them up to her chin, blushing scarlet.

David made no comment. 'I thought you might like this,' he said in the same clipped tones he had used the previous evening. Turning the mug carefully, he offered it to her handle-first.

'Th-thank you,' Gena's hand was trembling so much she had to use both to hold the coffee, and that meant dropping the bedclothes, which fell to her waist. Her baggy nightshirt, styled like a man's pyjama jacket, was a more than adequate cover, yet she was acutely aware of her nakedness beneath it.

'You look like a boy in that thing,' he observed suddenly.

'I feel the cold,' she countered, and her defensiveness made her angry. It was none of his business what she wore, in bed or out of it. Her hands shook even more and she was terrified she would spill the coffee, but there was nowhere to put it down. 'You should have called me,' she blurted. 'I had no idea it was so late.'

He shrugged. 'You obviously needed the sleep, and I have a healthy regard for my own safety.' At her quick frown he added, 'Who wants to fly with an overtired pilot? By the way, how *do* you feel this morning?'

'Fine,' she said at once, and realised it was true. Physically, the night's rest had completely restored her. She had been too exhausted even to dream. *And mentally?* She refused to probe. Work. She must concentrate on work. 'What are the plans for today?' Gena sipped the coffee.

David took a couple of steps back and leaned one elbow on the tall chest of drawers. 'That rather depends on you.' He gestured towards the window. 'Can you fly in this lot?'

Gena glanced at the window. 'Yes.'

'The rain is supposed to ease later, but there are more high winds forecast.'

'Then we'd better get going as soon as possible.' She was brisk and businesslike. 'If you'll excuse me . . . ?'

As soon as he had gone, Gena stumbled out of bed. His aftershave lingered on the air. A pair of pyjama bottoms were thrown in an untidy heap across his pillow. His wallet, electric razor, and a small travelling alarm clock sat on top of the chest. The room was full of him, even though he was no longer in it.

Within minutes she had dressed, made her bed and brushed her hair into a curly cap. After hurrying to the bathroom to wash her face and clean her teeth, she returned to the bedroom and quickly applied a light make-up. It helped reinforce the barrier she had resurrected and, as she sat down to breakfast, she congratulated herself. She had it all under control. Her emotional splurge had been an aberration, unfortunate but not irreparable. But it was over now, and the best thing was to pretend it had never happened.

David made it easier. He was obviously preoccupied, and the sporadic conversation, conducted by them both with painstaking politeness, widened the gap.

He insisted on drying their breakfast dishes as she washed. Once, as a plate almost slipped from her grasp and he caught it, their hands touched. The contact was an electric shock and Gena's heart gave such a kick she gasped.

'It's all right,' David reassured her, his voice oddly harsh. 'No harm done.'

Gena nodded, not trusting herself to speak. The plate was safe, undamaged. *But her?* The old saying, you couldn't miss what you'd never had, was a fallacy. Deep inside Gena ached. The barrier began to crumble and it took all her strength to hold it together.

By the time they got back from the hundred-kilometre round trip, having placed the last two outstations, the rain had stopped. Torn clouds raced across the sky revealing patches of blue. Then the sun emerged. But Gena was hardly aware of it.

As David climbed out of the Jet Ranger, he glanced back at her. 'Could you make lunch? There are one or two things I must do.'

'Yes, of course.' Gena said. 'What would you like?'

He shrugged, 'Anything. Perhaps you could open a can of soup? There are plenty in the cupboard.'

Gena nodded and watched his departing back. Yesterday he would have teased her and she would have defended herself, maybe got angry, and they would have laughed. *Yesterday.* Today, they were both walking on eggshells, so polite, so *distant.*

She switched on the cooker, opened a can of tomato soup and emptied it into a saucepan. Taking pitta bread and cheese from the fridge, Gena collected knives and spoons from the drawer in the sink unit, and carried the lot across to the table.

Returning to the cooker, she stirred the soup but, as she reached for the bowls she froze. It hadn't dawned on her before. She had been so immersed in trying to handle her own feelings, she hadn't had time to wonder *why.* Why had *David* changed? For he had. Gone were the banter, gentle mockery, and wide-ranging topics of conversation with which she had associated him since their moment of meeting. This morning, in fact since last night, he had been silent and withdrawn. When he did speak to her, it was with a pronounced air of strain.

She was certain she had not let slip the true extent of his fascination for her, the magnetic attraction which, in spite of her suspicion and defensiveness, drew her to him. Or was she deluding herself? *Oh, lord, had he guessed?* Had her feelings been so painfully obvious as to embarrass him into pointing out he wasn't free?

Humiliation crushed her. How could she look him in the face again? Yet what choice did she have? There was nowhere to run, no place to hide. She had to haul together the remnants of her pride and dignity, and carry on as though nothing had happened. After all, nothing had!

Noticing her discomfort, he had massaged her neck. That was all. A friendly gesture, nothing more. And how it had helped. She had heard of people with healing hands. She understood what that meant now. David had the gift, and she had been deeply, genuinely grateful.

Suddenly, in her mind's eye, she saw his face. 'Such games are dangerous,' he had said. But she hadn't been playing games. She had just felt so marvellous, and he had created that feeling.

He must have known what would happen when he started. It had been his idea. Unless . . . unless something had happened to *him*, something he had not expected, something . . . *No!* She must stop this speculation, this cruel, self-deceiving hope.

The door opened and he walked in. Her head jerked round. There was no time to compose her features. It was all there on her face, uncertainty, confusion, and desperate, hopeless yearning.

Their eyes met. He was utterly still for an instant. *He knew.*

He looked away to close the door. Gena placed the two bowls on the work-surface between cooker and sink unit with hands that trembled uncontrollably. Her heart was racing, hammering against her ribs with such speed and force she could scarcely breathe.

David came to the sink to wash his hands. Gena lifted the pan from the stove and poured the soup carefully into the bowls. Facing her, he rubbed his fingers dry with the towel. She turned the tap on to rinse the pan, and left it to stand in the washing-up bowl. He was so close.

Keeping her head bent, afraid to look up, knowing her thoughts would be all too visibly reflected in her expression, she could still see the lower half of his shirt, his slim hips and hard-muscled thighs outlined in olive-green cord.

It had not all been one-sided. He, too, was *aware.* The massage had been the moment of revelation. That was why he had warned her about dangerous games.

But she hadn't *been* playing. And she wasn't now. This was all too painfully real. She didn't know what to do, what to say.

He tossed the towel aside, but remained where he was, effectively trapping her in the alcove. It was deliberate. She would not, could not pretend she didn't realise. 'Gena?' he muttered, his voice harsh and throaty.

Slowly, helplessly, she raised her head. His dark eyes burned as he lifted his right hand and touched her cheek lightly with his fingertips.

Gena's lashes fluttered down. This is wrong, her conscience warned. But her body thrilled to his touch, every nerve exquisitely sensitive, vibrant, *alive.*

A shadow fell across her closed eyelids and David's breath fanned lightly over her face as, like petals dropping from a flower, his lips brushed hers.

A powerful urgency gripped Gena, making her shudder, and a barely audible sound issued from David's throat as his mouth sought and covered hers in a deep, searching kiss. His arms encircled her, drawing her to him.

Her hands rose to clutch at his shoulders. Then her knees turned to water as a strange vibration shivered up-wards through the floor. For a split-second she thought his embrace was responsible. Then she realised.

Her eyes flew open and in the same instant David straightened up, his head half turned, listening intently.

The vibration stopped. It had lasted barely three seconds.

'Was . . . was that another tremor?' Gena whispered, hardly daring to breathe. She knew it was ridiculous, but she felt that if she spoke too loud she might somehow make it worse. The thought flew through her mind that if she had to die, there was no better way to go than in the arms of this man. *But please, not yet.* She had only just begun to live, and she wanted more, so much more.

David released her. 'Mmm,' he said absently, his forehead furrowed, clearly thinking hard.

Gena rubbed her upper arms and tried to smile. 'It's a bit unnerving. I'm used to thinking of the earth as solid rock; now suddenly it's behaving like jelly.'

'Look, you go ahead and have your lunch,' he commanded, and started towards the door.

'What about you? Where are you going?' The questions were out before she could stop them.

'I have to rig up a test to calibrate the network.'

'But—'

He didn't give her a chance to say more. 'I'll eat later.' He was curt, tossing the words over his shoulder. He strode out, leaving Gena staring after him, suddenly cold.

Was it really work that called him? Did the tremor mean an earthquake was imminent? Or was his abrupt departure for another reason?

Was he regretting the kiss? A kiss was just a kiss. No, it wasn't, not between them. Now she understood his warning about dangerous games. He had a wife.

They were playing with fire, and she wanted, oh, how she wanted, to bathe in the flames. The touch and taste of his mouth had catapulted her into the realm of experience and sensation that was entirely new, and she wanted more. She yearned to explore him.

Even as these thoughts sped through her mind and she became aware of the disappointment, perplexity and tension that had tightened her muscles again, part of her was shocked. It was as though she was sharing her skin with a stranger. She didn't recognise the passionate, sensual woman who had invaded her mind and body. What was happening to her?

She looked at the soup, now rapidly cooling. Though the events of the past few minutes had taken the edge off her hunger, common sense told her she had to eat. If she wasn't careful, the added strain of emotional upheaval would deplete her reserves of strength and stamina more quickly than she could replenish them.

Putting David's meal in the fridge, Gena forced down soup, bread, cheese and fruit. She did the dishes and tidied the kitchen. She wandered into the bedroom and, not at all sure she was behaving sensibly, made his bed. She folded his pyjama trousers, stroking the material as if she could draw from it the warmth of his body. Then hastily bundled them under his pillow. She sorted out some undies and a shirt of hers that needed washing. Then, unable to find pegs, she hung them out to dry by threading them on to a length of string she found rolled into a ball under the sink. She tied it from the window mesh to the rail outside the door. The wind's raw edge made her shiver, but the sun was warm on her upturned face.

Restless, oddly on edge, she got out a book and settled down to read, telling herself she was *glad* to be alone, to have some time to herself. But after reading the first page three times and *still* not absorbing a single word, she flung the book aside. Rummaging under the sink, she found a plastic bucket and a scrubbing brush.

Half an hour later, tired and sweaty, her shirt sticking uncomfortably to her back, Gena rested on her heels. The floor was several shades lighter. Her fingertips resembled pallid prunes, all white and wrinkled. She sighed and dropped the cloth into the bucket. But, before she could get up, the door opened and David strode in.

'What are you doing?' he demanded, frowning.

'Isn't it obvious?' she retorted, getting stiffly to her feet and picking up the bucket. 'I'm praying.'

'What I meant was, I want you to take me twenty kilometres down the valley.'

'Then that's what you should have said,' she replied crisply. 'When do you want to go?'

'Right now.'

'I'll empty the bucket and get my jacket. May I ask why?'

'Certainly,' he replied blandly and, taking his jacket from the hook, put it on as he strode out again. Gena heard him go into the receiver-room, then the front door banged and his boots clattered on the steps.

Very funny. She could ask, but he wasn't bound to tell her. She wished there was something she could kick to vent her frustration.

Was he being deliberately provocative? Or was he just teasing, paying her back for her sarcasm? He had looked startled to see her scrubbing the floor. Why? she thought savagely. He must be used to seeing women on their knees. Weren't Muslim women little more than slaves to their menfolk?

But she wasn't Muslim. She was English, from a privileged background. She was intelligent, independent and highly qualified. So why, in heaven's name, was she having to scrub floors to try and get him out of her mind?

Gena closed her eyes and leaned against the sink, rubbing her forehead with her fingertips. Helplessly, she began to laugh. It was either that or weep. The whole situation had been complicated enough before. But now . . .

'Are you going to tell me?' she demanded as the base receded into the distance behind them.

'Tell you what?'

'It would help if I knew where we are supposed to be going,' she replied with exaggerated patience.

'I did tell you. Twenty kilometres down the valley.'

'Yes, but *why?*'

'I'm going to set off an explosion.' He might have been telling her he was taking the dog for a walk.

*'What?'* Gena instantly corrected the Jet Ranger's sideways lurch caused by her reflex jerk on the pedal.

He turned towards her. 'I have to calibrate the system,' he explained. 'All the stations must be on the same time-base.'

She glanced at him and, as their eyes met, she made a wry face and shook her head.

'I'm not making myself clear, right?'

She shrugged ruefully. 'This is all very new to me.'

'Please don't apologise.' His tone was drily amused. 'I'm amazed at your progress.'

His deliberately ambiguous phrasing, and the teasing note, brought her head round in suspicion. He raised one dark brow, his expression half-innocent, half-ironic. Hot colour flooded Gena's face. He had not been referring to her grasp of geophysics.

111

Instinctively retaliating, she flung the helicopter into a series of swoops and side-slips that forced him to cling to his seat.

'Sorry,' she sang airily. 'Turbulence. You were saying? About calibrating the system?' she added deliberately. This was not the time or the place for anything remotely personal. She needed all her wits about her.

His eyes were narrowed and thoughtful as they met hers. 'The method we use to find out where in the earth's crust a seismic event has occurred—by the way, that is the term we use to describe an earthquake.'

'Thank you,' she replied sweetly, inclining her head.

'The method,' he repeated firmly, 'is to measure the time it takes for energy waves from an event to reach the sensors.'

'Those are the boxes of instruments you set out yesterday and this morning?'

He nodded. 'For example, the first shock-wave in an event, the primary or push-wave, will travel at between six and eight kilometres a second, depending on the rock formation.' He paused and she sensed he was ordering his thoughts.

'If we know how fast the energy waves travel, and how long it takes for each sensor to register the waves, either electronically on a special tape-recorder, or visually on the paper roll graphs, we can work out not only where the focus of the event is, but at what depth.'

Concentration furrowed Gena's forehead as she tried to absorb all he was telling her. 'What's so important about the depth?'

'The deeper the focal point, the more widespread the damage. There was a quake in Alaska in 1964. That was a deep one. In fact, it was the most violent ever recorded. It completely demolished not only the town of Anchorage, but an area of over a hundred and thirty thousand square kilometres.'

'A hundred and thirty *thousand?*' Gena gaped at him. She could not even begin to imagine what it must have been like. Her experience of a very minor tremor had been unpleasant enough. But David hadn't finished.

'The slippage was so great that roofs on one side of the main street were level with the pavement on the other. Avalanches snapped huge pine trees like matchsticks. Oil storage tanks exploded and sent a great fireball across the town, and the railway lines were just a tangle of metal. That earthquake released the same amount of energy as one hundred and forty *million* tons of TNT. It rocked the seabed and created a wave sixty-seven metres high. The wave reached Hawaii six hours later and hit the coast of Japan nine hours after the event.'

Gena's eyes grew wider as she listened, her flying now automatic.

'B-but how long did the earthquake last? I mean, to do all that damage . . .' Her voice

113

tailed off.

'Not very long,' David answered grimly. 'Most last a minute or less. That's the point, you can't run away from an earthquake. An event in Morocco killed twelve thousand people in twelve seconds, and totally flattened the city of Agadir. But just one kilometre away there was no damage at all. The focus was shallow, you see.'

Gena nodded slowly. She started to speak, but her voice came out as a croak. She cleared her throat and tried again. 'What about here? H-have you any idea how—how deep . . . ?'

David shook his head. 'The geological formation is very complex.'

Gena moistened her lips. 'This explosion . . . it won't . . . will it? I mean . . .'

'It won't trigger off an earthquake, if that's what you're worrying about.' She detected both understanding of her apprehension and a glimmer of amusement in his voice.

She blew out a sigh of relief and grinned shakily, mocking her own reactions. 'Then why . . . ?'

David rested his elbow on the ridge where the plexiglass window met the metal door, and pushed a hand through his hair. It wasn't a gesture of impatience, more an attempt to gather his thoughts. 'To be able to pin-point the focus, I need to be sure of two things: one, that every out-station is functioning properly, sending back signals that can be recorded both

114

on tape and paper roll graphs. And two, which is even more important, that they are all registering from exactly the same point in time. Half a second difference between two recorders could mean an error of several kilometres. By creating an artificial event at a specific location and time, I can check backwards to make sure the network is registering accurately.'

'So, what do we have to do?' Gena asked.

'You don't do anything,' he replied curtly, 'except fly.'

'That's what I'm here for,' she retorted. 'Am I permitted to ask what *you* have to do?'

'Certainly.'

'Then tell me,' she persisted, her tone referring obliquely to his earlier behaviour.

'You really are interested?' His dry response held an underlying note of surprise.

'Are you serious?' Her voice climbed. 'I'm out here in the middle of nowhere, sharing a bedroom with a man I met two days ago, waiting for an earthquake—I beg your pardon—*event,* which this same man has blithely announced is *going* to happen, though he isn't quite sure *when,* and in the meantime he wants to blow up a valley for test purposes.' Running out of breath, Gena sucked in another lungful. 'Yes, you could say I'm interested. After all, this could be my last job. It's just possible something might go wrong. So under the circumstances, yes, I would like to know *exactly* what you intend doing.'

She tried to control her rapid breathing, and wished her heartbeat would slow down.

His laugh was deep and throaty, revealing white, slightly uneven teeth. It lit up his face and his dark eyes sparkled. 'Oh, Gena,' he murmured something in his own tongue.

'What does that mean?' she demanded suspiciously. His grin was broad, infectious, as he leaned towards her. *'Stop worrying.'*

She shrugged, her heart leaping erratically. He looked so different when he laughed, younger, and gut-wrenchingly attractive. 'Who's worried?'

He caught her eye. 'Well,' she muttered, 'it's different for you.' And reluctantly, the corners of her mouth flickered upwards.

David laid his hand briefly on her thigh. The fleeting pressure was, she knew, a silent gesture of understanding. There was nothing overtly sensual about it. Yet it sent her blood singing and her cheeks bloomed, warm and rosy. She prayed he wouldn't notice.

'How long before we reach twenty kilometres?' he asked, surveying the ground beneath them.

Gena glanced at the dial. 'A couple of minutes.'

'Once we reach the site, I have to do what is called field preparation,' he explained. 'In this case, all it means is that I bury the explosive.'

'Why?' Gena was curious. 'Why bury it?'

'If it's left on the surface most of the explosive's energy will disperse into the air. For the sake of the test, I want it to go down into the earth.'

Gena scanned the valley bottom. 'It's not going to be easy digging a hole in that lot.' She glanced at him once more. 'What sort of explosive do you use?'

'Standard blasting gelatine, the kind used in quarrying. Three sticks should be enough, strapped side by side with a detonator stuck in one of them.'

Gena was intrigued. She had forgotten all about her fear. 'Why do you need a detonator?'

He faced her and the teasing light in his eyes set her heart jumping again. 'How do you think I set off the explosive, Gena? Strike a match, light the blue touch-paper and run?' She blushed. 'One of the factors that makes blasting gelatine so safe to handle,' he went on, 'is the fact that it won't explode unless subjected to extremely high temperature. The detonator provides this.'

He swivelled round, awkward in his harness and the confines of the small cockpit, and reached backwards between the seats. 'I've got some here.' He opened a small flat tin, and held it where she could see.

Fascinated, Gena eyed the thin metal tubes, each half the length of a pencil, with two wires protruding from one end.

'You see the wires?' he pointed. She nodded, her attention divided between flying the helicopter and following all he was saying. 'They are joined by another length of wire to the exploder. And before you ask,' he raised his voice just as she opened her mouth, grinning as she glared at him, 'it's just a small box with a winder handle which is cranked to produce and store an electric charge. Once the gelatine and detonator are in place—and I have retired to a safe distance,' he added drily, 'I simply press the button on the box. The electrical charge is released, it flows down the wire and ignites an explosive plug the size of a match-head in the detonator, which in turn causes the gelatine to explode.' He snapped the tin shut. 'That, as they say, is all there is to it.'

'What do you call a safe distance?' Gena asked guardedly.

He thought for a moment. 'How about a hundred metres?' he suggested, and, though there was no visible sign of it, she sensed that inwardly he was laughing. 'You can go further if you wish.'

Reckoning that David Halman valued his life just as much as she valued hers, Gena shook her head. 'No,' she announced airily, 'a hundred metres will be fine.' She looked at the dials again. 'That's it. We are twenty kilometres from base.' They both peered down as she brought the helicopter lower.

118

The valley bottom was a tortured mass of rock. Gena scanned the rubble from innumerable landslides and the jagged edges of massive boulders split asunder by summer heat and winter snows, and shook her head. 'Sorry, David, it's impossible. I can't land on this. I might have managed it on wheels, at great risk to the tyres. But with skids it's out of the question.'

He didn't seem concerned. 'OK,' he decided, 'we'll follow the same procedure we used for placing the stations. Only this time, as soon as I've got everything out, you back off a hundred metres and wait.'

Twenty minutes later, her muscles beginning to quiver from the strain of maintaining the aircraft in a hover, Gena saw David straighten up from the mound of rubble and dirt he had piled over the gelatine. Tucking the shovel under his arm, he began making his way over the rock and debris towards her, unrolling the wire behind him as he went. But his progress over the broken ground was painfully slow.

Swinging the Jet Ranger forward, Gena brought it down to within four feet of the ground just skimming the serrated edges of rock that formed part of the ridge heaved out of the earth's crust more than a million years ago by forces too powerful to imagine. Her skin crawled and, swiftly, she diverted her thoughts to David.

119

'Throw the shovel in the back,' she shouted, pantomiming the action in case he could not hear above the engine's roar and the swish of the rotors. 'Sit inside, and feed the wire out through the open door.'

He gave her a thumbs-up.

Within a few minutes the wire was laid. Gena kept the helicopter hovering just above and behind him, while David, his hair wildly ruffled by the down-draught, attached the wire to the terminals and cranked the handle. She saw the light come on, a tiny red glow amid the shadowed rock. David glanced up at her, and raised his hand, thumb and forefinger joined in a circle to signify all was well.

Unable to reply, both hands needed for the lever and stick to hold her position, Gena nodded.

David pressed the button. There was a dull *crump*. The mound heaved. Dust and rock blasted into the air and, though prepared for it, Gena felt the shock-wave lift the Jet Ranger.

David hauled the passenger door open and clambered in, tossing the box and the remainder of the wire on to the back seat.

Before he had finished fastening his harness, Gena had swung the helicopter round and was heading at top speed for the base.

As the skids touched the ground, David leapt out and ran to the cabin. He took the steps in one bound and vanished inside, the door slamming behind him.

Infected by his urgency, pausing only to scribble the necessary figures in the log, Gena scrambled out and followed.

Closing the outside door and throwing off her flying-jacket as the cabin's warmth hit her, she hesitated briefly outside the receiver-room. Turning the handle, she slipped inside, almost tripping over David's jacket where it had fallen from the back of a chair standing in front of a desk strewn with books, graphs, and sheets of paper covered in figures.

Automatically picking up his jacket, she dropped it on to the chair and gazed round, her eyes widening. Needles flickered across the white- or green-lit dials of an array of electronic equipment which hummed softly. A long bench on which stood three tape-recorders, all linked to an electric clock, ran the length of one wall. On the opposite wall six roll graphs turned slowly, their recording pens making scratching sounds as they flickered across the pink and white paper.

His back to her, David was busy at what looked like a sophisticated tape recorder and amplifier. He looked round suddenly, and Gena flinched, wondering for an instant if she should have knocked before entering.

'Come here.' He motioned her forward. As she moved the few steps to his side, he pressed several buttons, then straightened up. His arm slid around her shoulders, drawing her closer

121

to him and to the machine. 'Listen,' he said softly, and flicked a switch.

All Gena could hear was the hiss and crackle of static. His arm was warm and heavy across her shoulders.

Suddenly, from out of the blur of sound came a dull thud, then another slightly softer, and another, fainter still. David's fingers tightened on the top of her arm as her head flew up.

'We did it?' Gena ventured.

David flipped another switch and the static's roar diminished. He smiled down at her. 'We did it,' he confirmed. 'Look,' he turned her so she could see the roll graphs, and pointed to the spiky trace, where the recording pen had suddenly shot half-way across the graph. 'There it is. The system's working perfectly.'

'Congratulations.' She smiled up at him, loving the sensation of his arm around her, exhilarated at sharing his success.

'Teamwork,' he said lightly. His eyes gleamed as they held hers. 'And now,' he said softly, 'we're ready for the real thing.'


## CHAPTER SIX

Gena's stomach lurched dizzily and her legs felt suddenly weak as tiny flames of sweet sensation licked her nerve-ends. Once again he had chosen words that could be interpreted in two different ways. A brief, searching glance, a swift meeting of eyes, told her it was deliberate.

She wished she could ignore that faint but insistent warning bell. It was impossible. He was married. He belonged to someone else.

He would never know what it cost her as she pretended a delicate shudder and grimaced. 'I'm not in a hurry.'

'No?' He tilted her chin with a forefinger. A quizzical smile lifted one corner of his mouth, but his dark eyes were serious as they searched hers. 'Considering . . . everything—' was it her imagination, or had he given that last word special emphasis? '—I thought you would be anxious to get back as soon as possible to normal life.'

*Normal life?* Was that what she had been leading before coming out here? Before meeting this big, impatient, humorous, fascinating, gentle, mysterious, *frightening* man.

'N-not if it means I have to take part in an earthquake—sorry, *event,* first.' She strove to keep her tone light, but already the atmosphere between them was subtly changing, becoming charged.

While they were working they teased and bantered, they lost their tempers and were blunt and honest, both confident in their professional skills. But once out of the emotional protection of working under pressure, when the job was all that counted . . .

Her heart began to race. She could feel his body warmth, smell his faint, musky man-scent. There was no pressure in the arm that encircled her. There was nothing to prevent her stepping back, away from him.

But she couldn't move. His touch was like a drug, paralysing her even as every cell in her body quivered with awareness, awakened to vibrant new life. She could feel herself trembling from head to foot. Surely he must know?

'Is there no one waiting for you back in England?'

Despite his casual, almost teasing tone, she sensed it was not an idle question. The tip of her tongue darted out to moisten paper-dry lips. Lie to him, common sense instructed. Put an end to this futile charade. There is no future in it. *He* has a wife. Tell him you too are committed.

She swallowed and shook her head. She couldn't lie. Maybe there was no future. Maybe the earthquake would solve the problem by removing them both, she thought wildly, choking back an hysterical giggle. But deny to herself this incredible new discovery? This amazing, glorious, anguished insight? She couldn't do it. 'Only my father.' Her voice was husky with strain. She attempted a shrug. 'And he will be far more concerned about the helicopter. But I've lived with that knowledge

124

a long time.'

'What about your engineer?' His tone was strange, reluctant yet forceful.

Bewilderment drew her brows together as she looked up. 'Jamie? What about him?'

David's throat worked, and a tiny muscle jumped at the point of his jaw. 'Is he your lover?'

For an instant Gena thought she had misheard. He *couldn't* have said . . . but his steely gaze and taut features told her she had not been mistaken.

Stiff with fury she tried to wrench herself free but, anticipating her move, he tightened his grip, clamping her against the hard length of his body.

'Answer me,' he commanded in a voice that made Gena think of broken glass.

'For pity's sake,' she cried, livid with anger and disgust, helpless in his vice-like grip, 'Jamie is married. He and Helen love each other very much, and I'm deeply fond of them both.' David looked startled, as though she had said something totally unexpected. 'Now, let me go,' she hissed.

He released her at once and she stumbled backwards.

'I—I'm sorry.' He sounded shaken, dismayed by his own behaviour. He reached out to her with one hand, but let it fall as she flinched back, rubbing her upper arms where his strong fingers had bitten into her tender

125

flesh.

'I thought you . . . he . . . I thought there was something between you.' His expression was deeply perplexed.

'There is,' Gena flared at him. 'Friendship. But maybe you're not fortunate enough to know what that is.'

Hunching his broad shoulders, David pushed his hands deep into the pockets of his cords. 'In my country, friendship between a man and a woman is not . . . common.'

'I'm not surprised,' Gena retorted, clasping her arms defensively across her trembling body, on the verge of inexplicable tears.

'No,' he insisted, his voice low, intense, 'you do not understand. In much of Turkey women are still subservient to men. First fathers and brothers, then husbands order a woman's life. The Koran calls it protection.'

'What do the women call it?' Gena didn't even try to disguise her antipathy. But, as he lifted his head and his eyes met hers, she glimpsed in their depths a bafflement which took her totally by surprise. Despite her efforts to hang on to her hostility, like snow in sunshine it melted and drained away. Bereft of protection, vulnerable once more, Gena waited.

'In my country,' David continued, 'we are encouraged to marry young. Once a man has a wife, other women should not exist for him.' He paused and half turned, gazing out of the nearest window into the purple dusk.

Gena studied his profile, the deep forehead, strong, straight nose and chiselled mouth. A mouth which, when smiling, could enchant, but when thin and hard with anger—goose-flesh erupted on her arms. Yet as she watched him there was no sense that he was wrestling with his conscience, or the defiance of a man intending to break the codes of his people, only this strange confusion she did not understand.

'In America,' he went on, so softly he might simply have been thinking aloud, 'it is different. There women dominate. They seem to see men as enemies or competitors. In their preoccupation with freedom and equality they deny the fundamental integrity of their sex, and behave in the very same ways for which they despise men. There is no winner in such a war.' He swung round suddenly to face her. 'You are right. I do not know this . . . friendship of which you speak.'

'David,' Gena began uncertainly, 'what made you think . . . why did you ask if . . . about Jamie?'

He raised his head, his eyes glittering like jet beneath the heavy brows. 'Don't you *know?*' He sounded surprised and slightly sceptical.

'Know *what?*' she demanded in exasperation.

He shook his head. 'It doesn't matter.

127

Perhaps I am seeing things that aren't there.'

Gena felt a sharp pang. 'That's something we're all guilty of from time to time,' she murmured.

'I think—' he began, then stopped. She looked up to see him studying her with a peculiar intensity. Her heart skipped a beat and she was suddenly breathless.

'Yes?'

'I think . . .' he repeated, and then she sensed a withdrawal, and knew he would not say what he had originally intended ' . . . we must eat now.'

Gena glanced at the clock. It was well after six. Her disappointment was smothered by a gasp of realisation. 'Oh!' Her hand flew to her mouth. 'You never did get any lunch.'

\*　　　　\*　　　　\*

Glowing from the hot shower, wrapped in a pink woollen dressing-gown over her nightshirt, Gena switched off the small hairdryer she always carried when travelling, and ran her fingers through her cropped curls.

As she replaced the plug with that of the kettle, David came in from the bathroom, rubbing his head with a towel. He was clad only in pyjama bottoms, his feet pushed into the backless sandals he used as slippers.

Gena turned away quickly. But the sight of his powerful body, swarthy-skinned and corded with muscle, the dark, curling mat of hair arrowing across his flat stomach, still filled her vision.

'Coffee?' she croaked over her shoulder, careful not to look directly at him as she reached up into the cupboard.

'Please.' He hooked the towel around his neck and started towards her. 'Can I help?'

'No.' She shook her head vehemently. She did not want him near. The urge to reach out and touch him, to feel the warm, smooth texture of his skin, to slide and curl her fingers in that black, silky mat, was almost uncontrollable. 'It's all done.' Her voice sounded husky and she swallowed hard. The kettle began to boil.

From the corner of her eye, Gena saw David rake his hands through his damp, rumpled hair in a casual effort at tidying it. 'To an outsider this would appear a very cosy domestic scene,' he murmured, as if simply musing aloud. 'You making supper, both of us freshly bathed, ready for bed.' He caught her eye. Behind the wicked, teasing gleam she glimpsed something else. But, before she could recognise it, he had reached past her, picked up his coffee and turned away.

She caught her breath, inhaling his scent, the faint musk overlaid by soap. Warm already, she flushed deep rose and turned her back on him, stirring sugar into her mug with a hand that trembled.

'Th-that just goes to show how deceptive appearances can be.' Gena tried to inject a no-nonsense firmness into her voice, but his words and proximity had kindled a strange urgency in her bloodstream.

'In what way?'

Slowly she faced him, leaning back against the sink, clutching her coffee mug in both hands like some sort of protective talisman. David had folded his length on to one of the easy chairs. He dwarfed it. Leaning forward, cradling the mug in his strong fingers, he rested his elbows on his parted knees.

'This is a working environment, not a home,' Gena said, 'and we are virtual strangers.' She tried to squash a sense of rising desperation. 'Any one of Brady Air Charter's pilots could have got this job. It was purely a quirk of fate that it fell to me.'

'Fate, destiny, call it what you like,' David's steady gaze pinned her to the spot, 'it sent *you* here. Not a man, not even another woman, but *you*, Gena.'

Then fate had a streak of malice, Gena thought, fighting the bitterness which threatened to overwhelm her. And yet—despite the fact that nothing could come of their meeting, would she rather *not* have met him? It was an impossible question. For peace of body and mind the answer had to be yes, and yet she had never felt so alive, never before looked so hard at her reasoning and her opinions. In the past two days she had learned so much, mostly about herself. Because of him her whole life had changed. It was like a rebirth. It hurt and she could not see a happy ending, but did she, could she regret it? *No.*

'Well,' she attempted a smile, 'that just proves my point. As you have discovered, I'm not at all domesticated.'

'Men do not marry for a housekeeper,' he responded drily.

Gena stared down at her coffee, her body prickling with sudden heat at the implications of his remark. This was getting out of hand. He had warned her about dangerous games, yet what was this? It seemed he was trying deliberately to torment her.

To gain time she raised the mug to her lips and drank. The hot liquid gave her strength. Tilting her chin, unconsciously defiant, she asked, 'What are the plans for tomorrow?'

One dark brow climbed, telling her he recognised her anxiety to change the subject.

Bravely, Gena held his gaze, moulding her expression into one of polite enquiry.

David unfolded himself from the chair and stood up. 'We're going to the nearest village. It's about ten kilometres over the mountains on the south side of the valley.'

As he approached, Gena quickly swallowed the last of her coffee and moved to the sink to rinse her mug. 'Why?' she asked over her shoulder.

'When the base was first established we had a lot of trouble with the villagers,' David explained. 'They saw us as intruders, which we were, and though the ground up here is just bare rock, they were afraid that if they didn't make a stand, other bases might be set up nearer them, using land on which they rely to graze their sheep. Pasture is sparse and precious up here.'

Gena was still, mug in one hand, drying cloth in the other, both momentarily forgotten. 'What kind of trouble?'

David shrugged. 'Vandalism, and theft. They smashed windows and stole anything they thought they could sell.'

Gena nodded slowly. 'I wondered about the metal grilles.' She watched David turn on the tap to rinse his own mug. 'What made them stop?'

'I did,' he said simply.

'How?'

'I went to see the head man. Every village has one, and his word is law, often the only law. Here in Eastern Turkey many of the villages are at least three days' horseback ride from the nearest town. The villagers might make that journey only a few times a year. Politics and sophisticated society are incomprehensible to them, so they have developed their own social structure. It's very basic, but it works.'

'Men do as they want and women do as

132

they're told?' Gena suggested.

He flashed her a look that acknowledged her irony. 'Something like that,' he agreed drily.

'It must have helped, you being half-Turkish,' she observed, putting the mugs in the cupboard. 'I don't only mean being able to talk their language. Knowing their ways and customs, you could explain things in terms they would understand.'

'It was useful,' he conceded. 'But when you are dealing with people who revere courage and love a fight, reasoned discussion has its limitations. A display of force often settles a problem with far greater speed and efficiency.'

Gena's eyes widened. 'What did you do?'

He folded brawny arms across his chest. 'The national sport in Turkey is wrestling. In my youth I was area champion,' he replied calmly. 'The head man chose three of the strongest men in the village and we fought. I beat two of them and saved the head man's face by losing to the third.' He shrugged. 'The head man promised the base would be left alone and I thanked him with a transistor radio and a watch. The villagers were only too pleased to have an excuse for a celebration and the rest of the day and night were spent drinking, dancing and playing *Cirit oyunu*.'

Tingles ran up and down Gena's spine at the mental picture David's laconic description had invoked. There were as many facets to this

133

man as a diamond.

'Wh-what is *jereed oyunoo?*' she stammered, struggling to get her tongue around the Turkish words, trying hard, and failing, to banish a vivid image of David, semi-crouched, muscles taut, his bronze skin gleaming with oil and sweat, poised to unleash his powerful strength in an explosive blur of movement.

'It's played on horseback. Wooden javelins are thrown at horsemen of the opposing team to gain a point. Except that it is not a team game in the English sense. Basically,' his mouth twisted in a sardonic grin, 'it's every man for himself. We Turks are fiercely independent.'

'Oh, is *that* what you call it?' Gena retorted.

'What would *you* call it?' he challenged at once, his eyes gleaming in a way that made Gena wish fervently that she had kept her mouth shut.

But though common sense, coupled with an awareness of her own vulnerability, warned her to be tactful, stubborn pride demanded she tell the truth. 'Arrogant?' she suggested. 'Dictatorial? Imperious? Overbearing?'

He gazed at her for a long moment and she teetered on the edge of panic, then his mouth widened. 'Could be.' He lifted one muscular shoulder in the suggestion of a shrug. 'But a man must do what a man must do.'

She knew he was teasing her again, and the now familiar magic began to weave its potent spell.

He glanced down at her hands. Following his gaze, she swiftly untwisted the drying cloth and hung it on the rail above the worktop beside the sink.

'So.' She swallowed. 'Why are we going to the village?'

David rested one hip against the sink unit. 'Partly to explain about the test explosion, and partly to warn them about the earthquake.'

Gena nodded. 'Well,' she announced with a brightness that rang horribly false, making her cringe inwardly, 'it looks as though it will be a pretty full day.' Wiping her palms nervously down the sides of her dressing-gown, she began edging past him. 'I think an early night . . . for me, I mean,' she added quickly, too quickly.

His hand snaked out, fastened on her arm, and drew her inexorably towards him.

Gena caught her breath. 'No,' she pleaded, her voice a hoarse whisper, her body stiff with resistance, fighting her own hunger and yearning as well as him.

His eyes burned like black coals and his face reflected his want of her. 'Why, Gena? Why do you fight it—me? It is a mutual attraction, we both know that.'

'Yes,' she admitted, the word torn from her, 'but it's impossible.'

'*Why?*' He seemed bewildered. 'I know it is sudden, but we have much in common, you

135

and I.'

'Oh, yes,' she cried bitterly, 'indeed we do, but there is one very significant difference. I suppose if it doesn't worry you, I should be able to ignore it.' She shrugged helplessly, then shook her head. 'But I can't. I've seen other people try, I've heard all the reasons and I've seen the grief and suffering behind brave faces. It's a situation I just can't handle.'

He let go of her arm at once. His features were stonelike, and shutters had slammed down behind his eyes, leaving them totally devoid of expression. 'I see.' His voice had a hollow ring. 'My apologies.'

Gena sensed something terribly wrong. It confused and angered her. He was married, he had told her so. He had no right to be hurt, yet he was. She could tell, despite his façade of cold politeness. Her rejection had wounded him deeply. *How dared he?* Didn't the vows he had made mean anything to him?

Perhaps a Muslim marriage did not place the same restrictions on a man as the Christian ceremony. Yet he himself had said that once a man married for him other women should no longer exist.

'Don't look like that!' She clasped her arms around her body, holding in her pain and confusion. 'If you really cared about *me* instead of being so concerned with what *you* want—' She broke off, knowing the accusation unfair, and turned her head away, unable to bear the torment and fierceness in his eyes.

'I was under the impression,' he said carefully, 'that something very special was growing between us. Am I wrong?' The sudden bewildered uncertainty on his face and in his voice tore at Gena's heart like a rusty nail.

'No!' It was a cry of agony. 'But we won't be here indefinitely, and what happens when we have to leave? Goodbye and thanks? It was fun while it lasted?'

'Gena, please, it doesn't have to—'

She shook her head, refusing to listen. 'That may be OK for you, but I can't . . . I'm not that sophisticated. I need—deserve—more, and under the circumstances,' her lips quivered, 'it is impossible . . .' The lump in her throat threatened to choke her. 'Excuse me,' she whispered and, head down, ran blindly to the bathroom. When she emerged he was nowhere to be seen.

That night Gena slept badly, tossing and turning. Nightmares mirrored her misery and distraction. She was haunted by a sense of loss, and in each splintered dream David appeared, angry and accusing telling her she had made a dreadful mistake.

*But she hadn't. How* could she embark on an affair with him, knowing it could last only as long as they were here?

Jamie managed, a small voice pointed out.

It was different for men, her consciousness

argued back. They could treat physical desire and love as two entirely separate things.

And you can't?

*Not with David.* Realisation jolted her awake and her eyes flew open to the primrose light of a cloudless dawn. Her gaze was drawn to the other bed. She saw at once it had not been slept in. She sat up, listening for the sound of movement next door. The silence was profound.

Scrambling out of bed, Gena hastily dragged on her dressing-gown and hurried, barefoot, to the door, the nameless anxiety generated by her nightmares intensifying to panic.

Snatching the door open, she stopped in mid-stride. Wearing a sweater over his pyjamas and half-covered by a blanket, David lay sprawled across the two easy chairs, still sound asleep.

There were shadows beneath the thick fringe of lashes. Yet he looked younger now the harsh lines of strain had been smoothed away by unconsciousness.

For the first time, Gena sensed a vulnerability in him that matched her own. It shook her. She gazed at him, fighting an almost overpowering urge to fall on her knees beside him and cover his face with kisses, and to hell with the consequences.

His eyes opened and he looked straight at her. Her heart lurched at the naked hunger

138

she saw in their depths. Then, like a curtain falling, all expression vanished and she was looking at a stranger.

'Is something wrong?'

The cool tone of enquiry made her start. was just going to ask you the same question,' I—I,' she stammered. 'Are you all right?'

'Perfectly,' came the terse reply.

'Only you didn't come to bed . . .' The words trailed off and Gena's face flamed.

'I was busy. There were two more minor tremors last night and I had a lot of calculations to work out.' Still holding the blanket around him, David stood up. He looked very tall and utterly remote. 'I would like to leave for the village at about twelve, if that is convenient?'

'Yes, of course.' Gena felt totally out of her depth.

'I have some maintenance work to do first.'

'Do you need any help?' she offered.

He shook his head abruptly. 'You mentioned rigging up some sort of anchor for the helicopter. As the gale warning was repeated last night, I think it would be wiser if you concentrated on that.'

And keep well away from me. Though he didn't say it, the implication was only too clear, and Gena felt the rebuff like a slap in the face.

The formality she could understand. They still had to share the same roof and were dependent on one another's professional skills. In difficult circumstances, courtesy oiled the wheels. But today there was a new hauteur about him. A bitter hurt that seemed out of all proportion. After all, what had she done except turn down an affair with a married man? It didn't make sense. Yet, if that wasn't the cause, then what was? A band of tension tightened round Gena's skull. Whatever his reason, the David she had known had withdrawn behind an impenetrable barrier.

During the rest of the morning Gena worked with feverish concentration. Rummaging in the store connected to the back of the cabin by a covered way, she found rope, chain and metal spikes. As she hammered the spikes into the ground, sweating in spite of the icy wind, her emotions seesawed between the gnawing fear that somehow, somewhere, there had been a terrible misunderstanding, and bitter anger at David for behaving as though it was all *her* fault. For pity's sake, *he* was the married one.

The village nestled in the fold of a hill, half-way down a shallow slope at one side of a wide valley still patchy with snow.

The ground around the stone-built houses was muddy and rutted, and chickens pecked in the dirt. Hay was piled high on several roofs, making the houses look as though they were wearing untidy wigs.

'Insulation?' Gena asked, breaking the long

silence as she pointed.

David nodded. 'And to keep it out of reach of the animals.'

A small herd of goats nibbled at patchy scrub, watched over by a group of children. Behind the village, the hillside was dotted with sheep.

As Gena brought the helicopter in to land, people began to appear. The women, all dressed in long skirts and woollen cardigans, their heads covered, emerged in ones and twos from different houses. But the men all seemed to come from one larger building.

'Is it some sort of workshop?' Gena asked.

David's smile had little humour. 'No. It's the *kahve,* the coffee house. Even the smallest village has one. In winter the men and boys spend most of their time there, playing cards or backgammon, drinking coffee and talking.'

Yesterday, the temptation to tease him, to make some pointed remark about the division of labour between men and women, would have been irresistible. But today . . .Gena made no comment.

As the helicopter settled, David unfastened his safety harness. 'Perhaps you would prefer to return to Ahslan and collect me later?'

Startled, she looked round at him, but he did not meet her gaze. 'No, I'd rather stay.'

'You will be the focus of curiosity,' he warned.

Gena shrugged. 'That's nothing new.'

'No one here speaks English,' he pointed out, 'so you won't know what's going on.'

'Can't you translate for me?'

He shook his head. 'Women are not permitted to enter the *kahve.*'

'Then I'll just have to manage on my own,' she retorted.

'Why bother?'

It wasn't so much the question, more the bitterness in his muttered tone that made her wince. Without stopping to think, she responded with the truth. 'Because this is your country and these are your people.'

His head jerked round and their eyes clashed, his glittering with an anger she didn't understand, hers wide with dismay. She hadn't meant to let that slip.

'Party chat for when you get home?' he bit the words off. 'Life among the peasants?'

'*No,*' she protested, but David was already half-way out. He slammed the door behind him.

A grizzled-haired man with a luxuriant black moustache and a three-day growth of stubble marched importantly towards the helicopter. The rest of the villagers formed a wedge behind him. He wore a very old, shabby, shapeless brown suit over an open-necked white shirt and a patterned woollen pullover.

As David went forward to greet him, the man began waving his arms about. Gena wasn't sure whether he was actually angry, or simply excitable.

Replacing the log-books, she climbed out and locked the door behind her, then pulled on her flying-jacket and zipped it up. The air was as clear and sharp as chilled wine, and her breath condensed into a small cloud.

Not quite sure what she was supposed to do, she stretched her mouth into a smile and started forward, hand extended, to greet the head man, who stopped in mid-tirade to regard her with total incomprehension.

David glanced swiftly round, and caught her arm, jerking her to an awkward stop. 'No,' he murmured firmly.

'What?' Gena bristled. 'I was only being polite.'

'In England, yes,' David grated, 'but not here. Now stand still and keep quiet, or go back to the helicopter.' Not giving her a chance to reply, he switched smoothly to Turkish.

Gena's embarrassment grew as she saw that behind their hands and veils, the women were talking about her. Sibilant whispers reached her ears. There were smothered giggles and disapproving murmurs as eyes that gleamed like raisins observed and dissected her from her coppery head, down her leather jacket and flying-suit, to her fleece-lined boots.

Her discomfort was further heightened by the realisation that the men too were scrutinising her, some surreptitiously, others with a boldness that made her want to hide behind David.

Angry with them, and with herself for feeling unnerved, she tilted her chin defiantly and stared back.

'Gena?' David sounded impatient.

'What?' She looked up at him. His face was expressionless, but there was a curious light in his eyes.

'I said, the head man is asking if you are my wife. What shall I tell him?'

Was he being deliberately cruel? She moistened her lips. 'The truth. I am not your wife.'

His gaze was penetrating. 'Are you sure that's what you want? It might cause problems.'

'Not half as many as if we lie,' she murmured.

'Don't count on that,' he warned.

She raised her chin. 'I have never hidden behind a man yet, and I don't intend to start now. Tell him the truth.'

He held her gaze for a moment longer and she sensed a battle raging within him. 'As you wish,' he said at last. He turned from her and answered the head man.

With a collective intake of breath the women drew back, and the whispers increased to a buzz.

Gena touched David's arm. 'What is it? What are they saying?'

'It doesn't matter.' He was brusque.

'Tell me,' she demanded.

'All right,' he almost snarled. 'Any woman sharing a roof with a man to whom she is not related, either by blood or marriage, is regarded as a whore.'

Gena felt the blood drain from her face. 'Is that so? They, of course, don't know that I did not choose the arrangement.'

'If they did it wouldn't make any difference,' he said bluntly. 'We are living together.'

'No, we are not,' Gena hissed vehemently. 'Not in the sense they mean.'

'You think they'd believe that?' His voice was harsh. 'We make a striking couple, Gena. Though clearly you don't see it that way.'

That's not true, she wanted to shout at him and, in a desperate effort to stem the flood of denials, bit the inside of her lower lip so hard that she tasted blood.

'And you?' she challenged unsteadily. 'I suppose your honour is still intact.'

'This is very much a man's world.' Though his tone gave little away, his eyes held swift compassion.

'So you told me.' With an enormous effort she kept her voice steady. 'I think I'll go for a walk. I brought my camera. I won't embarrass the villagers by attempting to photograph them,' she added, the casual façade slipping to expose her distress.

'Their objection would not be personal,' he

said quickly, 'but religious. The Koran forbids the portrayal of the human image.'

'Oh, I see. Fine. Enjoy your meeting.'

'Don't stray too far from—'

'I'm not a child, David,' she gritted.

'You're not armed either,' he retorted at once, 'and there are wolves in these hills. Why else do you suppose the shepherd boys carry rifles, and their dogs wear collars studded with metal spikes?'

'And you wouldn't want to lose your pilot.' She knew she was being unfair, but she couldn't help herself. She *hurt*.

'That's right.' The cold, clipped tone rubbed salt in the wound. Her vision blurred, Gena turned on her heel and walked away.

Faint sounds of shouting and cheering drifted towards her on the freshening wind. Gena glanced at her watch. It was over an hour since she had left the village. Turning her collar up, she glanced skyward. A thick mass of charcoal-grey cloud was moving across the sky, the wispy, ragged leading edge indicating strong winds. The air smelt different, dank and raw, and Gena wondered with a sinking feeling if they were in for one of the infamous spring blizzards she had been warned about.

Retracing her steps, she rounded a curve in the hillside and looked down into the wide, flat valley bottom.

Men on horseback were galloping to and fro at a furious pace. Every few moments a rider would stand in the stirrups, one hand on the reins to control his mount's headlong dash, the other raised to throw a wooden javelin at a rival who weaved and ducked to avoid being hit.

One rider caught her eye. Taller than the others, and hatless, he rode like the wind, his horse seemingly an extension of himself. Drawing his arm back and whirling his horse into a tight turn, he waited for the right moment, then hurled the javelin. A roar of approval went up as it struck its target.

Well, that was the test explosion taken care of, she thought wryly. But as she watched him gallop back to his own side and pick up another javelin, she felt a peculiar pain in her chest.

'David,' she whispered. 'Oh, David, why you?' In so many was he was still a stranger, yet she felt closer to him than anyone she had ever known. There was a bond between them, an intuitive understanding which could neither be denied, nor openly acknowledged. Why was life so cruelly unfair? How could she take her happiness at some other woman's expense?

*Need anyone else know?*

The thought startled her. She had been so definite, so determined to do the right thing.

*What harm would it do?* While in no way pressuring or rushing her, David had made no secret of his attraction to her. His commitments were *his* business, not hers. She was free.

*And when it was time to leave?* Maybe they would both be quite content to go their separate ways. The itch would have been scratched, their hunger satisfied. No strings, no tears. All neat, tidy—and utterly impossible. A lifetime would not be long enough.

She knew, with as much certainty as she knew her own name, that never again would she meet anyone like him. There *was* no one else like him. He was his own, unique self, a blend of western sophistication and warrior Turk, of science and sport, of intellect and physical prowess. And behind an incisive mind and dry humour lay an unsuspected defencelessness. She was falling in love with him.

Her hair tumbled by the rising wind, she held her collar over her ears, her eyes following his every movement, drinking him in. 'Oh,' she whispered, her breath clouding the cold, turbulent air, 'what am I to do?'

## CHAPTER SEVEN

Deeply immersed in her thoughts, Gena did not notice the three young men loitering in the shadow of some rocks.

As she wrenched her eyes from David, and turned along the hill towards the helicopter, the three stepped out of their shelter, making soft clicking sounds with tongues and teeth.

It took a moment for the sounds to register. Then Gena stopped, her head lifting, eyes wide, unfocused, as she tried to gather her wits.

Catching sight of the young men, her first reaction was a polite nod and a half-smile. It was automatic, what she would have done at home.

Only she wasn't at home. She was in an alien country whose customs and beliefs were very different from those she was used to.

As the men exchanged glances, and edged out across her path, placing themselves between her and the helicopter, Gena realised with a sinking feeling that, once again, she had done the wrong thing. She should have ignored them, pretended they were not there.

But they were. And they were blocking her way. So what did she do now?

She remembered reading a police warning to women caught in threatening situations to keep their heads lowered as eye-contact was often interpreted as deliberate provocation. Yet all her instincts, and her self-esteem, screamed at her to look directly at the men, challenging their right to stop her, cutting them down to size with a contemptuous glare and some biting words. Though they would not understand the language, the tone and sense would be crystal clear to them. But the warning kept coming back, and there were three of them.

Her own uncertainty was draining her courage. She felt weak and helpless, and hated the feeling. Keeping her eyes lowered, she changed direction slightly, heading further up the hill, willing them to go away and leave her alone.

It wasn't until she heard the shuffling sounds of their shoes on the loose stones and risked a swift glance that she realised her mistake.

While one of them still blocked her path, the other two had placed themselves between her and the crowd watching the game at the bottom of the valley.

Gena's heart began to beat faster and unease trickled like ice-water along her veins.

One of the men, who appeared to be in his early twenties, unshaven, his clothes grubby, his teeth stained brown by tobacco, called something to her in a soft, low voice. The other two snickered.

Gena stopped and looked up. She shook her head firmly. She had not understood the words, but the suggestive tone had been unmistakable.

The men merely laughed, and began to close in on her, exchanging remarks between themselves, encouraging one another. They kept asking her questions, their eyes hot and glittering, and the accompanying obscene gestures made their intentions all too clear.

Gena flushed scarlet with embarrassment and rage. 'No,' she said fiercely, making a cutting movement with her hands. 'No. Don't you understand?'

Their fading grins, deepening frowns and growing irritation showed that they understood *what* she was saying, but not why she was saying it.

Gena seethed. They were behaving as though she had no right to refuse. Maybe their women had no choice, but she wasn't one of *their* women, and they knew that.

Issuing terse instructions to his companions, the man facing her unbuckled his belt and pulled it free of his trousers. Wrapping it around his knuckles, he started towards her. The other two began closing in, one at the side, the other moving around behind her.

Raw panic flooded through Gena. Barely conscious of what she was doing, she opened her mouth and screamed David's name with all the power in her lungs.

The men looked startled, then, muttering among themselves, their faces lighting up with leering grins, they lunged forward.

Trying to watch all three at once as she scrambled backwards up the hill, Gena screamed once more for David, her voice cracking with strain and fear.

*He couldn't hear her.*

Suddenly Gena realised that if she kept

going backwards, *up* the hill, she was lost. The men were cutting her off from the village, the helicopter, and from David.

They were closing in, no longer hurrying, taking their time, enjoying the sport. Their expressions were changing as well, growing avid. Excitement burned in their eyes and they licked their lips as their voices grew coarser and more guttural.

Gena stopped her scrambled retreat. Drawing herself up, she stood for an instant, tall and perfectly still, balanced on the balls of her feet.

The men were taken momentarily by surprise and hesitated. As they started forward again, Gena sucked in a deep breath. Screaming at the top of her voice, she launched herself straight down the hill.

The man directly below lunged forward, trying to stop her, but she flung her arm out to fend him off and felt a wild thrill of savage satisfaction as her fist caught him full in the face and with a strangled shout he sprawled full-length on the snow-streaked ground.

This time her shriek had caught the attention of some of the crowd. And to her utterable relief she saw David's head turn. He seemed to read the situation at a glance.

Leaving the game, spurring his horse into an even faster gallop, he cut through the spectators like a knife through butter.

Skidding on loose shale and patches of

snow, terrified she might fall, but not daring to slow down for fear of being caught, Gena hurtled down the slope.

Fear lent wings to her feet. She could hear the stones slithering, and the pounding of footsteps. Her breath was an agonised rasp.

David leapt from his horse and swept her into his arms, swinging round with the force of her momentum.

'Don't let . . . catch . . . they . . .' she gasped, incoherent, her lungs heaving with exertion and fright.

'It's all right,' David murmured, but the soothing words had an oddly rough edge.

Gena clung to him, trembling uncontrollably, partly from reaction and partly from the physical effort of her headlong sprint. 'B-but they were going to . . . they would have . . .' Her voice quivered and tears of rage and relief spilled over. 'I thought you hadn't heard me.'

'It's over now,' David grated. 'Nothing happened.'

Gena's head jerked back. 'Nothing . . . ?' she panted. 'Is that *all* you have to say?'

Grasping her upper arms, he shook her, clearly fighting to control the emotion that seethed in him. 'In the name of all that's holy, what did you expect?' he snarled. 'I warned you, but you wouldn't listen. This is not a tourist area. The people here do not tolerate western ways. But you insisted on *honesty*. You have no one to blame but yourself.'

Gena winced under his tongue-lashing. And, though she wanted to fight back and argue, she had to admit he was right. 'Whatever happened to the concept of respect and protection for women?' she murmured wearily.

'A woman wearing a man's outfit?' David's eyes raked down her flying-suit. 'Doing a man's job? Speaking before she is spoken to?' His tone was harsh. 'What sort of woman is that in these people's eyes?'

'All right, you've made your point.' Despite her efforts, her voice had a definite wobble. 'Please, do you think we could leave now?'

David released her. 'No.'

Gena's teeth began to chatter as shock took hold. Her eyes widened. 'Why not?'

'It would appear to be a rejection of hospitality.'

She stared at him. 'I don't believe this. What hospitality have I been offered?'

David's expression was stony. 'You got exactly what you asked for.'

'What the hell do you mean?'

David's eyes glittered like chips of black ice. 'If the head man had believed us to be married, you would have received only deference and respect. Those same three men who wanted to rape you would have guarded you with their lives. But you refused.' The terrible edge of bitterness in his voice cut

Gena to her soul. 'You reject my protection. You deny what you *know* exists between us. Yet whose name is on your lips at the first sign of trouble, trouble which you have invited?' His contempt was lacerating.

Once more confusion overwhelmed her. How could he pretend it was so simple? She had no right to the kind of *protection* he offered.

David turned away and started towards his horse which was cropping the sparse grass a few yards down the hill. The three men had vanished. Either they had melted into the crowd, or had taken the chance while her back was turned to return to the village. But, once David left her side, what then? Gena felt her resolve harden. She was not going to risk the same thing happening again.

'David?'

He glanced back over his shoulder.

'We have to leave now. I'll wait for you in the helicopter.'

Slowly he turned to face her, his features darkening at her defiance.

'Th-the weather is deteriorating.' Though she held his gaze without flinching, her heart was beating a frenzied tattoo against her ribs. She didn't feel she could take much more. She was hungry and cold, and fear had taken its toll on her nervous system. She *had* to get away from here.

David looked up at the fast-moving clouds.

Full-bellied and fuzzy-edged, they were already obscuring the mountain tops.

'Look, we really do have to go now,' she said desperately. 'It's going to snow before nightfall.'

'It's only ten kilometres to base,' David reminded her. 'We will be back in plenty of time.'

'I'd agree, if that was the extent of my journey,' Gena said carefully. The idea had only just occurred to her. It was the answer to her prayers.

David frowned, his eyes narrowing. 'What are you talking about?'

Gena swallowed. 'After I've dropped you off at Ahslan, I shall fly on down to Van.'

*'Tonight?'* Her announcement was clearly a shock to him.

She nodded, trying to keep her face expressionless. She hadn't planned it this way, yet it made such good sense.

She needed to get away. Away from this village, away from David Halman. She needed a chance to get things in perspective, to know what she really felt.

No, that wasn't true. She knew only too well what her feelings were. She had to decide what she was, or wasn't, going to do about them.

More than anything she needed space and solitude, and she would find neither at the cabin.

'I—I hadn't planned to go just yet, not for a

few days,' she admitted. 'But if the helicopter is going to be grounded by a spell of bad weather, if I'm in Van, at least Jamie can be getting on with the servicing.'

'Ah, yes,' David's mouth curled in a grim half-smile. 'Jamie, the faithful friend.'

There was a note in David's voice that Gena didn't understand. She was about to ask him what he was driving at, but before she could frame the words he told her curtly that he would be with her in five minutes.

The journey back to Ahslan was made in silence. It was an uncomfortable flight with a lot of turbulence due to the thick cloud and gusting wind. As well as the storm brewing outside the Jet Ranger, Gena also had the upheaval within herself to contend with. She wanted to e-plain why she needed to get away, but couldn't find the words. In any case David seemed unreachable, absorbed in his own thoughts.

'You should eat before you go,' he said, tossing his jacket on to one of the easy chairs as he crossed to the sink to fill the kettle.

'There won't be time.' Gena made straight for the bedroom. Hauling her bag out from under the bed, she took her nightshirt from under the pillow, rolled it up with her dressing-gown, and stuffed it into the bag. She added clean underwear, a fresh shirt, a pair of socks and her hairbrush.

Pulling the second drawer open, she stared

down at the neat folds of her long skirt and pretty top. It was only a few days since she had worn them, yet it seemed like a lifetime. Leaving them untouched, she slammed the drawer shut and, dropping the bag outside the bedroom door, hurried to the bathroom for her face-cloth, soap and toothbrush.

As she returned to the kitchen, David held out a mug.

'Drink it now, while it's hot,' he directed. 'I'm making you some sandwiches. You can eat them while you fly.'

'There's no need . . .' she started to protest, but he cut her off with an explosive mutter in Turkish.

The barely controlled violence in his voice and manner made her flinch. He glared at her. 'Is it so hard to accept anything from me?'

Startled, she blinked. She hadn't meant it that way. But, as she opened her mouth to stammer an apology, David's features hardened into a mask of aloofness.

'I would have done as much for any colleague. Don't run away with the idea that you are receiving special treatment.' His tone was caustic. 'I know how irritating you would find that.'

'No,' she began, 'I didn't mean . . . that wasn't . . .'

'You had better hurry.' He was brusque.

Gena felt as though she was being carried along by some juggernaut over which she had

158

no control. Now that David seemed almost anxious for her to go, she was having doubts. But it was too late.

Besides, her reasons for going—the weather, and maintenance for the helicopter—were genuine. A couple of days apart was the best thing for both of them. It would disperse some of the emotional tensions.

Gena zipped up her bag, swallowing the last of her coffee, and carried her mug to the sink to rinse it. David was wrapping the sandwiches.

'All being well, I should be back by lunchtime the day after tomorrow,' she announced, drying the mug with concentrated care.

'I'm not going anywhere,' came the laconic reply.

There was nothing more to keep her. As she picked up her bag and her jacket, David placed the packet of sandwiches in her hand. He didn't let go, forcing her to look up. 'Make sure you eat them, Gena. There's a lot of adrenalin in your system right now. Add low blood-sugar and fatigue, and you are inviting trouble.'

'I won't forget,' she whispered, helpless in his piercing gaze. 'Th-thanks.'

Unexpectedly, he touched her cheek with his forefinger. The gesture was so full of restrained tenderness that Gena's heart flipped over. The silence stretched and, as he studied her with a strange intensity, a muscle flickered at the corner of his mouth.

'What if I tell you that the army can bring me out? That you need not come back at all.'

She stiffened. That was the *last* thing she had expected him to say. He was standing so close. She could feel the magnetic pull of his body. He radiated strength and warmth, and it enveloped her like a cocoon. Strain tightened the back of her neck as she raised her eyes to his. She cleared her throat. 'Are you firing me?'

'No,' he said, his voice low and harsh. 'I am giving you an option. If you consider the risks are too great . . . the *professional* risks . . . Your father is holding you responsible for the helicopter. The choice between risk of damage and completing the contract can only be yours.'

He was giving her a way out, a legitimate, criticism-proof escape clause. She could leave now and simply not come back. They need never see one another again. Under the circumstances, wouldn't that be the most sensible course of action?

'I—I'll give it careful thought,' she murmured, her mind reeling. *Never to see him again?*

He nodded. 'You do that.'

They gazed at each other a moment longer, neither willing to break the contact. Then, with a muttered curse, David crushed her to him, his strong hands moulding her body against his as if he would absorb it into his own.

His mouth covered hers in a kiss that betrayed the turbulence raging inside him. His lips parted hers, ruthless and demanding. But, as his tongue explored the soft inner contours of her mouth, the kiss changed to a silent cry of need, hunger and loneliness.

With the clarity of a star-shell bursting, Gena recognised in David's kiss a reflection of all the things *she* was feeling. And when a few moments later he raised his head, his breathing swift and ragged, eyes cloudy with desire, Gena was clinging to him, deafened by her pounding heartbeat, her body seared by their passion, her vision blurred by the sparkle of tears.

David turned his head and took a step back. Grasping her upper arms, he held her firmly away from him. His fingers tightened for an instant, then he released her. He strode to the door and wrenched it open. 'Get the hell out of here,' he grated.

The sound of the outer door slamming behind her still echoed in Gena's ears as she wound the engine up and prepared for take-off.

Choking back sobs, fiercely scrubbing away hot tears with the heel of her hand, she went through her pre-flight checks. The pain was physical, agonising in its intensity. She had to go, yet she was leaving behind part of herself.

She wanted him so much, but he was already committed to someone else. He was a part of this country. He understood it. He belonged. She did not.

As the helicopter lifted off, she could not resist one last look at the cabin, a swift, searching glance combining hope and despair. But the door remained closed, and behind the mesh screens the windows were blank, like unseeing eyes.

Within five minutes the first snowflakes hit the wind-screen. There were only a few to begin with, tossed like feathers on the wind. But they rapidly increased, becoming an opaque, moving curtain.

Locked inside the swirling blizzard, Gena was flying solely on instruments. But she had set her course, and as she checked her altitude, direction and airspeed the Jet Ranger carried her away from David, the valley and the earthquake, eastward to the town of Van and the familiar, comforting presence of Jamie.

As soon as she was within radio range, Gena called the airport and asked that Jamie be paged. She needed him there the moment she arrived. Whether she went back to Ahslan or returned home to England, the aircraft would have to be serviced. But, more than anything else, she needed a friend.

She flew out of the blizzard and into the brilliant sunshine of a late spring afternoon, over valleys lush with trees and grass, the verdant green a balm to her eyes after so much barren rock, over tilled earth and sprouting crops. The vast expanse of Lake Van glistened like a sheet of blue glass beneath her. A field of red poppies, their heads bobbing in the breeze, was a splash of vivid colour against the grey rock that edged the shores and, to the north, snow mantled the rounded summit of Mount Süphan.

'All right,' Jamie demanded, squeezing her hands. 'I want the truth. Has Halman been giving you trouble?'

They were standing on the concrete apron, watching ground crew push the Jet Ranger into its allotted space in the huge, brilliantly lit hangar workshop. Around them the airport buzzed with activity. Large aircraft arriving and small aircraft leaving on the last of the day's internal flights, taxied along runways. Fire tenders, lorries carrying freight, and trailers loaded with luggage, trundled to and fro. Engines roared, horns peeped, doors slammed, people shouted to one another and hurried about on important errands.

'Gena?' Jamie tugged at her hand. 'Has he?'

'No.'

'You don't sound very sure.'

Gena pushed a hand through her hair. 'It's—it's all been a bit confusing.'

'Has he upset you?' Jamie's face was livid. 'If he's hurt you, I'll take him apart. Bloody arrogant foreigners, they're all the same'

'Hey, hang on a minute.' Gena frowned, perplexed. 'What on earth is the matter with you two? Jamie, when I left Erzurum at the beginning of the week, you were telling me to "spread my wings". I was ready to fly, you said. You were practically throwing me at David Halman.'

Jamie looked down at his feet. 'Yeah, I know,' he muttered. 'I meant it then, too. The only trouble was, I didn't realise . . .' He shook his head as though dismissing the thought, and drew her hand through the crook of his arm. 'So,' he attempted a cheerful grin, 'what are you doing down here? You weren't due back for at least a week. Is the bird running rough?'

'No, and never mind that for the moment. What do you mean, you didn't realise? What didn't you realise?'

'Look, it doesn't matter.' He avoided her questioning gaze.

'Yes, it does.' Gena was determined. 'There's something you both know about that I don't. David has been making cracks about you, referring to you as my *faithful friend,* and his tone was anything but admiring. Do you know, he had the gall to ask if you . . .if we . . .' She flushed and shook her head. 'Well, never mind about that.'

'If we what?' Jamie demanded, pulling her round to face him.

'If we were—are—lovers,' Gena blurted. She looked bewildered. 'Where could he have got an idea like that?'

'What did you tell him?' Jamie's expression was curiously intent.

'The truth, of course,' Gena retorted. 'I told him that you were a very dear friend. I also told him you were married, and that I was very fond of Helen too. Which *is* the truth, isn't it?' She hugged his arm, expecting immediate confirmation.

Jamie placed his hand gently over hers. 'Part of it,' he answered carefully.

Gena glanced at him, clearly puzzled. 'What do you mean?'

Jamie raised his head. His eyes were full of sadness and a self-deriding smile twisted his mouth. 'Halman is no fool. He has eyes like the proverbial hawk. He knew almost at once. I didn't have to say a word. He told *me.*'

'*What,* Jamie? What are you talking about?'

He looked down at his hand half covering hers. Then, compressing his lips for a moment, he turned his head away. 'He recognised something I've tried to ignore, something I've tried to hide from myself. He saw . . .' Jamie cleared his throat, 'he saw that I love you. I've loved you for years. I dare say I'll go on loving you until I die. *No,*' he said sharply, his voice cracking as she made to speak. 'Don't say anything. Let me finish. We may as well get it over with.' He stroked the back of her hand with clumsy, shaking fingers. 'I never intended to tell you. I knew nothing could ever come of it. I can't leave Helen, and you're not the sort of girl to want a hole-and-corner kind of affair,' his mouth stretched in a travesty of a grin, 'assuming of course that you could ever think of me . . . that way.'

'Oh, Jamie,' Gena breathed, moved, awed and horrified all at once.

'Don't,' he blurted. 'Don't say anything,' he cut her off as she opened her mouth. 'It's probably just as well it's out in the open. I can't go on kidding myself. Those other women, you did understand about them? When you're hungry, you eat. When you're thirsty, you drink. They meant no more than that. I used to daydream that some day things might be different. That you and I could—' He shook his head. 'They say there's no fool like an old fool. You're not for me, Gena. You never were, never will be. I knew that the moment David Halman knocked on the door and asked for *Mr* Brady. Before then I'd cherished my dreams. But after . . .' He pressed her hand. 'Part of me wants to kill the bastard, but the other half knows it wouldn't make a scrap of difference.'

'Jamie—'

Still he would not let her finish. Stretching his seamed face into a brave smile, he jerked his head sideways. 'Come on, there's a canteen of sorts just the other side of the workshops. You must be starving. It's not every day you're faced with the confessions of an aircraft mechanic.'

She shook her head. 'I'm not hungry. I had sandwiches during the flight.' Sandwiches David had made, caring about her, knowing she was flying back to Jamie. Knowing Jamie loved her. She swallowed the tightness in her throat. 'But I'd give my right arm for a cup of tea. Do they serve tea here?'

'Only with lemon,' Jamie grimaced. 'No one has ever heard of making it with milk. And they call this the cradle of civilisation.'

As soon as they were settled at a small corner table, with Gena screened from general view and no longer the object of prying eyes and curious stares, Jamie began to question her again. 'So, what's the base like?'

She felt her face grow hot. 'Small. But at least it's warm and dry.' Now she was here, free at last to unburden herself, to spill out all her confusion and misery, something held her back. It wasn't just Jamie's startling declaration. Now she could understand David's scepticism. He must have thought it very odd that she had no idea of Jamie's feelings. But she hadn't had even a glimmer. Even now she found it almost impossible to believe she had actually heard the words he'd said.

'Any sign of the earthquake?' Jamie's mouth was grinning, but his eyes were full of strain and he was visibly tense, hunched forward over the table as he played with the spoon in his glass of tea.

'A few tremors, nothing too violent yet.' Gena felt strange. For an instant it was as though the geological upheaval, and the kisses she had shared with David, were interchanged.

'And Halman? Is he . . . is he treating you OK?' Jamie glanced up at her from under his brows, gripping the spoon so hard that his knuckles gleamed white.

'He's a strange mixture, Jamie,' Gena murmured, her head bent, eyes unfocused as images of David filled her mind. 'While we're working we get on really well together. The problems seem to start when we're *not* working.'

'What do you mean?' His voice was hoarse. 'What sort of problems?'

She shrugged uncertainly. There was so much she couldn't tell Jamie now. On top of everything else, David Halman had lost her her one true friend. 'Division of labour, for a start. He expected me to cook. It didn't go down too well when I told him I couldn't.'

'That's one of the things I always admired about you,' Jamie said softly, not looking at her. 'You had the guts to break out of the strait-jacket of tradition. You refused to accept limitations and restrictions just because you're a woman.'

Gena's smile was bitterly ironic. 'People change, Jamie. I'm not half as clever as I thought I was. I'm not even the person I thought I was,' she added softly.

'And this is Halman's doing?'

'I suppose he's partly responsible,' Gena admitted.

'Aaah,' Jamie sighed.

Gena looked up. 'What do you mean, *aaah?*'

'You've fallen for him, haven't you.' It was a statement, not a question, and his tone was hollow.

The pain pierced her like a stiletto blade. 'That would be an utterly pointless thing to do.' Her tone was sharper than she intended, but she couldn't bring herself to apologise. Jamie didn't have a monopoly on anguish. She took another sip of tea. It was lukewarm and slightly acrid.

'Why?'

'Oh, come on, Jamie. You know as well as I do.'

'You mean because he's half-Turkish?'

'No, of course not.' Gena was impatient, dismissive of something that seemed totally irrelevant. 'I mean because he's married.'

Jamie's face creased into a bewildered frown. 'What are you talking about? More to the point, what's *he* up to?'

'What do you mean?'

'David Halman isn't married. He was, but his wife is dead.'

Gena started so violently, her tea slopped over the rim of the glass, and ran between her fingers and down the back of her hand. *'What?'* she gasped.

'He's a widower,' Jamie repeated. 'His wife died three years ago.'

Gena replaced the glass on its saucer with a clatter and wiped her hands on the paper napkin Jamie passed her. Her thoughts were a mad whirl. She felt dizzy and light-headed. 'Are you *sure?* How do you know? Who told you?'

'He did.'

'He told you?' she repeated blankly. 'But . . . when? How?'

'Our last evening in Erzurum. The night before you both took off for Ahslan base.'

'But . . .' Gena's face mirrored her stupefaction. 'We all ate together. He talked about Turkish history. He never said anything . . . I *know* he didn't. We were talking about the job and about servicing arrangements here.'

Jamie nodded. 'That's right. But you went to bed as soon as we finished eating. Halman and I stayed talking over coffee.' He caught her eye and flushed brick-red. 'I guess I told him more than I realised.'

Gena shook her head wearily. 'He tends to have that effect on people,' she murmured. 'Go on.'

'Well, I can't remember how, but something came up about hospitals, it must have been a follow-on from talking about service facilities.

Anyway, I mentioned Helen and her accident, and that was when he told me about losing his wife. Apparently, it was one of those awful freak mishaps. She was only in for a minor op.'

Gena searched his face, her mind a whirling maelstrom of relief, uncertainty, guilt, hope and anguish. 'What happened?'

Jamie lifted his shoulders. 'He didn't say. Just that she died.'

*Then why had he told her he was married?* Gena's head felt as though it was about to burst. Resting her elbows on the table, she pressed the tips of her fingers to her temples.

Jamie's chair scraped on the floor as he stood up. 'Come on, I'll see you back to the hotel.'

She looked up and shook her head. 'No. I'm all right.'

'You don't look it.' Jamie was blunt. 'In my opinion, you need something to eat, followed by a hot bath and twelve hours' sleep. And what I need,' his grin was crooked and not very convincing, 'is to get on with the job I'm being paid to do.'

Gena didn't have the strength or the inclination to argue. These two latest shocks, Jamie's confession of his true feelings, and the revelation that David was not, after all, married, coming on top of the strain of the visit to the village, plus David's suggestion that she need not return, had pushed her to the limits of her endurance.

171

Jamie dropped her bag on to the bedcover and pushed the key into the lock on the inside of the door. He pointed to the paper bags she was holding. One contained spit-roasted lamb and a salad of tomatoes and onion rings in a pitta envelope, the other a feather-light pastry stuffed with nuts soaked in syrup. 'Eat your supper, then get some sleep. I'll see you tomorrow.'

'Th-thanks, Jamie, for . . . for everything.'

He waved her words aside, and though his head was turned towards her, he could not meet her eyes. 'I should have the bird ready to fly by four.'

Gena frowned. 'But . . . you'll have to work half the night . . .'

'Got any better suggestions?' he rasped, and immediately shook his head. 'I'm sorry. I shouldn't . . . I'm sorry, Gena.'

'It's OK,' she whispered, wishing she could help him and knowing there was nothing she could do.

'You'll be back at the base tomorrow night.' Jamie's voice was thick. 'That is what you want, isn't it?'


## CHAPTER EIGHT

*Was* it what she wanted? Incapable of further thought, Gena followed Jamie's orders. She ate her supper, soaked in a steaming bath, then crawled into bed and into oblivion.

Nine hours later, physically refreshed, Gena breakfasted on fruit, freshly baked rolls with cherry conserve, and Turkish coffee prepared in the traditional way, the fine powder boiled to a froth in a brass pot, and served with plenty of sugar.

Then she walked through the bazaar, lingering at stalls selling gleaming copper jugs, vases and trays, silver jewellery, brightly coloured rugs, lengths of material covered with magnificent gold-thread embroidery, and leather handbags.

She watched street vendors in their traditional costume of black shirt, baggy black trousers held in place by a broad striped sash knotted at one side, and a waistcoat richly embroidered with gold thread, selling bags of nuts and sweets from trays.

The fruit and vegetable stalls were a riot of colour, piled high with shiny purple aubergines, yellow melons, scarlet tomatoes, and red and green peppers.

Gena sat on a wall to rest for a few moments. A white cat appeared from among the stalls, padded on short legs towards her and leapt lightly on to the wall, rubbing its head against her arm.

She stroked the long, snowy fur and, as the cat looked up at her, purring loudly, she noticed it had one blue eye and one yellow.

173

'You're an oddity,' she murmured to the cat. 'That makes two of us.' She sighed. 'But at least you belong here. I don't know where I fit in any more.'

With a final nuzzle, the cat jumped down from the wall and disappeared among the legs of the crowd. Gena took a deep breath and walked on. While the surface of her mind noted her surroundings, the rest of her thoughts centred on David and the dilemma that faced her. Should she, could she, go back to the base?

Now she had time to think, and was no longer overpowered by David's physical presence and the need to control her own reactions and responses, she could give attention to the question hammering at her brain. *Why had he told her he was married?* Then her stride faltered as realisation cut through the clamour. *He hadn't.*

When she asked who had taught him the massage technique, he had answered, 'my wife'. That was all he had said. Those two words were a straight answer to a specific question. *She had assumed the rest.*

They had both been surprised and confused by the effects of the massage. Perhaps her question had reminded him of whatever tragic circumstances surrounded his wife's death. For his own reasons he had chosen not to elaborate. So the seeds of misunderstanding had been sown.

When she had tried to scuttle away to bed and he had stopped her, unable to hide his attraction to her, demanding she recognise it as mutual, she had fought him off. She had told him she couldn't handle the situation, meaning an affair with a married man.

But he had known he *wasn't* married. So what situation had he imagined she was referring to?

She saw again the deep hurt behind the stony mask. She saw his shock, his disappointment, and recalled his sudden self-protecting hauteur and disdain.

More images flashed before her glazed eyes. Faster and faster, they bombarded her from every side. His barbed scorn when she had said she wanted to learn about his country and his people; his caustic anger at her refusal to sidestep problems by telling the head man they were married; and his bitterness at her reluctance to accept his help as she got ready to come down here. What were they telling her?

The images spun together in a kaleidoscope of colour and movement and she closed her eyes in an effort to shut it out. Something was gnawing at the edge of her consciousness, something Jamie had said.

Then she remembered. When she had said that falling for David Halman was an utterly pointless thing to do, Jamie had asked, *Why? Because he's half-Turkish?*

175

She had been impatient, brushing the idea aside without even considering it. Her sole reason for rejecting David had been her belief that he was married and that any relationship between them could only be brief, furtive, and based on deceit. That was why she had seized the excuse offered by the deteriorating weather to escape from the cabin and the potent web of physical and emotional attraction entangling them both and drawing them inexorably towards the moment when denial of their mutual feelings and need would be impossible.

But David hadn't known she believed him to be married. He must have thought, *must still think,* that it was his background, the fact that he was of mixed race, which had caused her to reject him.

With a start, and an apologetic smile to a man on a bicycle with whom she had almost collided, Gena turned her back on the noise and bustle of the bazaar, and made her way in bright sunshine towards the old part of the city.

As she walked amid the quiet ruins of the mosques and mausoleums she forced herself to consider the question. *Did* his ancestry make a difference?

The answer was immediate and unequivocal. Of course it did. It made him the man he was, the man who had so profoundly shaken her, who had made her question all her

176

old beliefs and values. It made him the man who stirred her to the very depths of her being and kindled in her the yearning to be a total woman. It made him the man whose proud features, bronze skin and penetrating dark eyes took her breath away and sent tiny flames of erotic urgency licking along her veins. It made him the man she admired and respected, *the man she was falling in love with.* But would she be able to convince him that she cared for him *because of* and not in spite of his background? Was it even worth trying? His pain and pride had encased him in an armour which might prove impossible to breach. Why should he believe her? And what if he didn't? What if she went back and he continued to treat her with the scorn and disdain he had shown before she'd left? The atmosphere would be impossible. The cabin was too small for them to live separately, and the intensity of their feelings, the crackling electricity generated by their suppressed anger, resentment and desire could all too easily explode into violence.

He had offered her a way out, a reason that would satisfy her father and insure there was no claim on either side for breach of contract. Wouldn't it be more sensible to accept the fact that the chasm between them was too wide to bridge. That there were too many differences and had been too much misunderstanding? Surely she would be saving herself untold grief by accepting that this relationship could never come to anything? Yes, the attraction had been strong, more powerful than anything she had known before. But there had also been friction, false impressions and misjudgements from the moment they met. Why should it be different now? Besides, how much time did they have left? A week? Two? And what then? She had to return with the Jet Ranger to England and her next job. Who knew where David would be needed? He had to go where his work took him, and England ranked very low on the league table which showed frequency and magnitude of earthquakes.

Maybe her decision to fly down here yesterday had been for the best, after all. The most difficult part, actually leaving him, was behind her. He had given her the option not to go back. Obviously that was what he felt was best.

Gena sucked in a tremulous breath. He was right. It *was* for the best.

She made her way back to the hotel. All the warmth had gone from the sun. Birds twittered and sang, the pure, liquid sounds carried on a gentle breeze, but she didn't hear them. The mellow light seemed to draw from the ancient stones a richness of colour and texture that would have inspired any artist to reach for his paints. Gena was blind to it. It was as though, somewhere deep inside her, a new, tender blossom whose fragile petals were just

178

beginning to unfold had been seared by the icy burn of a killing frost.

She packed her few things, decided not to wear her flying-suit until it was time to leave, and went up to the rooftop restaurant for lunch.

She would have to telex her father and let him know she was on her way home. She would also have to devise some sort of message for David, confirming that she wouldn't be returning.

The food was like sawdust in her mouth, and the choking lump in her throat prevented her from swallowing any more.

The waiter hovered nearby, visibly concerned when she pushed her barely touched plate away. In an effort to compose herself, Gena sipped a few mouthfuls of *ayran,* a refreshing drink made from yoghurt whisked with cold water. The waiter disappeared, only to return a few moments later with the chef, who was clearly anxious to know what had displeased her.

By the time Gena had convinced them that the fault was entirely hers and nothing at all to do with the quality, cooking or presentation of the food, she was fighting back tears.

The hostility of the villagers had, in some ways, been easier to deal with than this care and concern, especially now she had made up her mind to leave.

By the time she had checked out of the

hotel and got a taxi to the airport, it was well after two. Jamie had promised to have the helicopter ready by four, which would give her ample time to send her messages, file a flight plan, and obtain clearance for refuelling at Malatya.

She would need to stay overnight at Ankara and fly on to Istanbul in the morning. If there were no hitches she could be back home by tomorrow night. *Home.* What did that word mean? An empty flat and no one to whom it really mattered whether she came back or not. Correction, she thought bitterly, it mattered to her father. She had in her care a large chunk of the company's assets.

Hearing her footsteps as she walked across the hangar, Jamie looked down from his perch half-way up a mobile platform. He replaced the spanner he had been using in the tool-box level with his hip, and wiped his hands on an oily rag.

'You're early,' he said gruffly. Gena nodded. 'Anxious to get back to Ahslan, I suppose.' His attempt at a grin wasn't successful.

Gena moistened her lips. 'I—I'm not going back.' Her voice revealed the strain which, despite all her logic and reasoning, was tearing her apart inside.

Jamie stared at her, his hands suddenly still.

Gena explained, 'David—Dr Halman said that the army could airlift him out when the job was finished. He—he told me to consider whether the risks to the helicopter . . .' She couldn't go on. Biting her lip hard, she struggled for control, blinking back scalding tears. Her chest hurt with the effort of holding in her grief. Telling Jamie made it real. She really was leaving. She would never see David again. 'Anyway,' her voice wavered and she sucked in a deep breath, 'I've given the whole situation careful thought and taking . . . everything . . . into account.'

'You have to go back,' Jamie announced flatly.

Startled, Gena looked up at him. 'What? What do you mean? I've just—you can't—' She shook her head.

Jamie dropped the rag on the engine cowling and came down the aluminum steps to stand in front of her. 'There's something you don't know. When I was on my lunch-break I got talking to the pilot of a charter flight that had just arrived from Elazig, due west of this town. He's carrying a party of culture vultures who are doing a tour of the archaeological sites in eastern Turkey. He was interested to know what I was doing here so I told him about the base, and about Halman's theory regarding the impending earthquake. He asked where the base was, and when I told him he looked worried. It seems that one of the nomadic tribes who winter in the lowlands with their sheep and goats have started their trek to the higher pastures. They are in the

Musgüney mountains, heading north-east, less than a hundred kilometres from Ahslan base. It's not just men and animals. They've got women, babies and young children with them.'

'Oh, dear heaven!' Gena whispered, her imagination already leaping ahead and recoiling from the vision. 'If the earthquake hits while those people are—'

'Exactly.' Jamie's expression was haunted. 'You have to go back, Gena. You must tell Halman.'

'But he can't stop the earthquake,' she cried helplessly.

'Of course he can't,' Jamie retorted. 'But he speaks the lingo. He can talk to those people, warn them to get out of the area as fast as possible. Gena, the only way he can reach them in time is by helicopter.'

His gaze was tortured, and she closed her eyes to shut it out as the battle raged inside her.

If she didn't go back and those people died ... could she live with that on her conscience? But if she *did* go back, she would have to stay and see the job through to the end, and that would mean not only twenty-four-hours-a-day proximity to David, but going through the leaving a second time. It was like tearing sticking-plaster from a wound. She had done it once. Heaven knew, it hadn't been painless, but at least it had been quick. If she went back she would have to do it all over again. The days would be difficult enough, *but what about the nights?*

He could not continue to sleep in the kitchen, nor would he, he had made that plain.

How glibly she had claimed that she slept well and nothing disturbed her.

'You have no choice,' Jamie grated. 'You *must* go back.'

Her head bent, eyes still closed, Gena knew he was right. Silently, she nodded.

'Right,' he said. 'By the time you have filed your flight plan and got a weather forecast, I'll have the bird ready for testing.'

'Thanks,' Gena whispered, and turned away.

'One more thing.' A new huskiness thickened Jamie's voice. 'I'm flying home tomorrow.'

Gena froze, then whirled round, her eyes wide.

'The boss has OK'd it,' he continued, gazing fixedly at his oil-streaked hands as he rubbed one with the rag. 'I told him I didn't think it was advisable for me to be away from Helen any longer. He agreed.' Jamie tried to grin. 'I guess he's been adding up the overtime and expenses I'm due. Anyway,' he swallowed audibly, 'I'm booked on the morning flight. If you're out here long enough for the bird to need another service, he said he'd send Ken Webster to take care of it.'

His gaze met hers finally and they stared at

one another. After a long moment, Jamie's shoulders moved imperceptibly. 'Goodbye, Gena,' he whispered.

With a strangled cry, Gena flung herself at him. Wrapping her arms around his neck, she hugged him with all her strength. She couldn't speak. There was nothing more to say, it had all been said.

Jamie had been her dearest friend and now he was leaving her. The next time they met everything would be different. A door was closing on part of her life, and though she knew it was inevitable, even necessary, she grieved for what was lost. She had never felt so utterly alone.

Tears squeezed between her tightly shut eyelids and her chest heaved with her efforts to control the sobs that shook her.

Jamie held her close for a few moments, rocking to and fro. Then he reached up, loosened her arms and, gripping her hands, stepped back, deliberately putting some distance between them. His own eyes were wet and his seamed face looked suddenly old and drawn. 'Be happy, lass,' he muttered. 'Life is precious. Don't waste it. You never know when . . .' He cleared his throat and with his next words his voice was stronger, more steady. 'Go and get your paperwork sorted out and let me finish up here.'

He gave her hand a final squeeze almost painful in its intensity, and she sensed all that he could not say. Then, releasing her, he turned away to clamber up the ladder once more.

Her teeth almost meeting through her bottom lip, her throat stiff and aching with unshed tears, Gena walked round to open the pilot's door. She tossed her bag on to the back seat. By the time she had climbed into her flying-suit, put her jacket back on and collected the wallet with all her flying documents in, she had regained a precarious control. There would be no more tears, she vowed. Their parting would be cheerful, full of the usual banter and teasing. She owed Jamie that much.

\*     \*     \*

The sun was setting behind the mountains in an angry blaze of orange and purple and, as Gena brought the helicopter down next to the cabin, an eerie light filled the valley for a few moments before fading so suddenly it was as though a switch had been thrown.

As the engine cooled and she wrote up the logs, her heart began to pound, the beat loud and rapid in her ears. She tried hard to concentrate on the figures, but her eyes kept straying to the cabin.

The door remained shut and there was no sign of his face at the windows. David had to be here. There wasn't anywhere else he could go without transport, unless . . . No, the earthquake could not have happened yet, there would have been something on the news. Somebody would have mentioned it. Besides, it was bound to take several days *after* the event to collect all the data and retrieve the instruments, and for that he needed a helicopter. The army? Not yet. It was too soon.

She switched off the power. The rotors slowed and stopped. Now Gena could hear the wind. It howled, screaming past the blades. Gusts nudged the aircraft, making it shake.

Outside, the noise was deafening. There would be a momentary lull, then, with a noise like an express train, it would roar down the valley. Snatching at her hair, moulding her clothes to her body, and forcing her to grab hold of something in order to keep her balance and not be carried forward. A shrill keening tore at her nerves and after a few moments she realised it was caused by the wind in the radio aerials.

Once she recognised the source of the sound, Gena dismissed it from her mind and concentrated on fitting and securing the sleeves on to the rotors to stop them whipping up and down. As she crouched to fasten her home-made shackles over the skids, her upturned collar shielded her ears and so she missed the faint *ping* as a wire parted on one of the stays holding the radio mast and all its

186

antennae in position.

She stood up, surprised to see that dusk had fallen. There were still no lights in the cabin. Apprehension dried Gena's mouth. *Where was he? Why was there no sign of life?*

Grabbing her bag from the back seat, she went up the steps and opened the door. The cabin smelled different. She couldn't immediately place the new smell and ignored it, more concerned with finding David.

After glancing into the receiver-room, knowing it was a waste of time, that he was unlikely to be sitting there in the dark, she closed that door and switched on the kitchen light. Dropping her bag on the cupboard under the window, she went to fill the kettle. Her throat was parched, and her nerves strained. She needed something hot and sweet to help her face whatever lay ahead.

She had just put the plug in and was reaching for her bag when the bedroom door crashed open. Gena spun round with a gasp as David stumbled into the kitchen. Seeing her, he froze.

She stared at him. Tousle-haired, unshaven, dark shadows beneath bloodshot eyes contrasted with a haggard pallor.

Deeply shaken by the way he looked, Gena said the first thing that came into her head, not stopping to think. 'Have you been drinking?' she blurted.

David's features tightened with swift anger.

In two strides he reached the coffee-table and snatched up the bottle standing on it. Swinging round, he lunged forward and held it under her nose. She recoiled, but he followed her.

'Smell it,' he ordered. 'What is it?'

Cautiously, not taking her eyes from him, Gena sniffed. Now she recognised the smell she had noticed on opening the door. 'M-methylated spirit,' she answered.

'Do you think I've sunk to that?' he demanded, his voice harsh, his tone ironic. 'How gratifying to know you have such a high opinion of me.' He put the top back on.

'Have you looked in the mirror today?' Gena hit back at once, her stomach churning with the upheaval of her mixed emotions.

'No,' he snarled, reaching past her to slam the bottle down on the cupboard top with a thump that made her flinch. 'As I have had only three hours' sleep since you left, my appearance hasn't been high on my list of priorities. And before you start leaping to any conclusions, the reason had nothing to do with you.'

Instead of being a comfort or reassurance, his words stung like a slap in the face. *As he had intended,* she realised.

'Well, that's a relief,' she said briskly. Only her pride kept her head high and her voice steady. 'So what was the problem?'

Closing his eyes for a moment, he rubbed his forehead. The utter weariness in the

188

gesture wrenched at Gena's heart, but she steeled herself against it.

'The generator failed just after you left and I couldn't get the reserve going. I had to use Tilley lamps for light to work by. They run on paraffin—oil,' his tone grew sarcastic, 'but guess what they are primed with?' Gena bit her lip. 'Well?' he demanded. 'Come on, genius,' he made it sound like an insult, 'you're always so quick with an answer. I'm sure you must have this one on the tip of your tongue. Any child knows that you use methylated spirit to light a primus stove or Tilley lamp.'

'*All right,*' Gena cried, 'you've made your point. I was wrong. I shouldn't have—' Her voice fell. 'I'm sorry.' She felt weak and shaky. This wasn't how she imagined it would be. There had been no clear picture in her mind of their reunion. She had known it wouldn't be easy to break through the barrier he had erected. But neither had she expected this pent-up violence that emanated from him, surrounding him with a force-field that was almost visible.

David leaned against the cupboard and, after running his fingers through his rumpled hair, he folded his arms and stared at the floor.

The kettle was boiling, filling the alcove with steam. Gena reached across to turn it off. With trembling hands she opened the cupboard above the draining board. Her stomach revolted at the thought of more coffee and she recognised that, with tensions running so high, stimulants were the last thing either of them needed right now. She took down a jar of chocolate-flavour malted milk powder. Holding it tightly in both hands, she turned to face him.

'D-David?' He grunted but didn't look up. Gena pressed on. '*I am* sorry. It was just . . . you looked . . . it was a shock. I guess if I'd been the man you expected, the generators would have been checked and serviced, and they wouldn't have broken down.' She shrugged helplessly. 'Or, if they had, you'd have had help to repair them.'

He rubbed one hand across his face, a gesture that spoke of more than physical weariness. His palm rasped against the growth of black stubble. 'Forget it,' he muttered. 'If you had been a man . . .' He shook his head abruptly. Raising his eyes, he pierced her with a burning gaze. 'Why did you come back?' His tone was raw, accusing, but beneath the harshness Gena caught the echo of her own pain, and a tiny spark of hope flared among the ashes of her dreams. Putting the jar down, she fetched mugs and spoons.

'Jamie told me . . .' she began, but at the mention of the name, David's mouth thinned and his features grew hard and cold. 'And how is your *friend?* Did you have a good time together? You were so anxious to get back to him.'

'Shut up!' Gena shouted at him, her hands clenching into fists. She was shaking with anger. 'Jamie Drew is—was—the only close friend I ever had. Coming from a big family, you won't know what that meant to me, how important it was. He was the one person I could rely on, the one person who really cared. He was the older brother I never had. Maybe I'm stupid and naïve, but it never crossed my mind . . . he never gave even the smallest hint . . . ! Tears spilled over her lashes and trickled down her flushed cheeks.

She gulped back a sob. 'He's flying home tomorrow. He has asked for a transfer. The next time we meet it will be like talking to a stranger; there'll be a bloody great wall between us. I didn't know he loved me. But I do now. You made sure of that. And it's destroyed something very precious.'

Gena closed her eyes momentarily, turning her head aside. *She would not break down.* She clasped her fingers, digging into her own flesh as if this small pain could somehow displace the larger one. She tilted her chin, her gaze scathing. 'You should be proud of yourself.'

His features were drawn and beneath the stubble he was pale. 'Jealousy is new to me,' he grated. 'I'm not proud of it.'

Gena's eyes widened. 'Jealous?' she repeated blankly. *'You?* Of *Jamie?'* But, before she could absorb all the implications of his statement, he was speaking again.

191

'What did he tell you that brought you back here?' He was visibly tense. His dark eyes burned. And suddenly, as though a veil had been lifted, Gena saw how close to total exhaustion he was.

Quickly she explained about the tribe. He listened in silence, staring at the floor. When she had finished, he looked up at her once more, his face expressionless.

'Let me get this straight. You came back in order to fly me out to warn those people about the earthquake?'

She nodded. 'It's too dark now, but we can go at first light.'

'Why didn't you call me on the radio?'

Gena stared at him for several seconds. 'It—it never occurred to me,' she stammered. It was the truth. 'In any case, what would have been the point? You need a helicopter to get across the pass to warn those people. I know you said the army could—'

'Wrong,' he cut in quietly. 'As far as that's concerned, I don't need either you or your helicopter.' Gena gaped at him, stunned. 'You forget, this base has been here for several years and there are others all over eastern Turkey. This is a known earthquake zone. Earthquakes cause landslides which often block the passes. We have a network warning system which not only includes the bases, but various points along routes traditionally used by nomadic tribes.'

192

'W-warning system?' Gena croaked.

He nodded. 'Flares. At the bases we fire them manually. But the outlying ones are operated by radio signal. The army replaces them after use. All civil and military aircraft regularly report tribe movements to the aviation authority who pass the information on to the bases in bulletins. I'll probably receive one in the morning.'

Gena turned away, shattered by what he had just told her. Clinging to the pretence of normality by going through familiar motions, she spooned malted milk powder into the mugs and mixed it to a cream with cold water. Gripping the kettle tightly, observing her shaking hand as though it belonged to someone else, she poured boiling water and whisked the drink to a froth.

She needn't have come back. Hard on the heels of that realisation came another. Jamie had known. If the pilot had told him about the tribe movements, he would also have told him about the warning system. But Jamie had deliberately doctored the story, telling her only half of it, knowing she could not under those circumstances refuse to return to the base. Loving her, he had sent her back to David. It had been his parting gift.

Gena caught her bottom lip between her teeth in an effort to still its quivering. Damn you, Jamie, she raged inwardly. He had had no right to interfere. But for him, she would be on

193

her way home now. Instead, looking a complete fool, she was once more alone with a man who was anything but pleased to see her.

Staring into the steaming mug, she cleared her throat. 'I didn't know about the flares and everything. I couldn't risk . . . Jamie said there were women and children. If the earthquake . . .'

'Is one of those for me?' he interrupted, gesturing at the mugs.

'What? Oh, yes.' Gena reached for the sugar bowl, intending to pass it to him. But it slid from her fingers, and caught the edge of his mug, which promptly tipped over. The hot liquid spilled across the draining board and dripped on to the floor where the fragments of the sugar bowl still rocked among the brown crystals.

Gena buried her face in her hands. 'I'm useless,' she muttered, totally crushed by the weight of humiliation and self-contempt.

'No.' David was thoughtful. 'You cared enough about those people . . . *my* people—' he corrected himself deliberately, but Gena barely heard him.

'I'll leave tomorrow.'

'You won't,' he said flatly. 'You're back and you'll stay.'

'What for?' Gena cried, glaring at him. 'What's the point?'

'*I need you.*' His retort, furious, anguished,

194

determined, hung in the air between them.

'B-but you said . . .'

'I know what I said,' he snapped, daring her to argue.

Gena held her burgeoning hope tightly in check, frightened to let it grow, terrified she might be wrong.

The silence lasted for several seconds, and in that time the atmosphere underwent a subtle change.

Gena looked up at him across the debris. She clasped her hands together, unconsciously twining and entwining her fingers. 'The warning aside, I presume you still need a pilot?'

The corners of his mouth lifted. It was a fleeting, crooked smile, but it was the first since her return and it made Gena's heart lurch.

'By your own admission,' he countered, 'you aren't the world's best cook.'

She hunched one shoulder in a helpless shrug, acknowledging the truth of his remark, then indicated the mess on the floor. 'I'm clumsy, too.'

'Who isn't, under stress?' he said softly.

Gena's throat was dry. She swallowed. 'Why I left,' she blurted, 'it was true about the weather and the service due on the helicopter,' she added quickly.

He nodded, almost impatient, but remained silent. She moistened her lips with the tip of her tongue. On the worktop, the remaining drink cooled, but Gena had forgotten it was there. His dark eyes seemed to penetrate her very soul. She wanted to look away but couldn't. Still he said nothing, waiting, forcing her to go on.

'I—I thought—I honestly believed—you were married.' His expression sharpened. 'I . . . I know now I was wrong, that you aren't, not any more.'

He searched her face. 'Jamie told you?'

She nodded, then looked up at him, her eyes wide, fearful, as an awful possibility dawned. Jamie had lied once to get her back here. Had he, thinking it was what she wanted, lied again? 'It—it is true, then?' she ventured, almost afraid to ask, for if it were not—she steeled herself for his reply.

'That my wife is dead?' he grated. 'Yes, it's true.'

Gena didn't know what to say. Convention dictated she offer condolences and sympathy. But how *could* she say she was sorry when her whole happiness depended on his being free?

As if David sensed her dilemma, his expression softened, making her aware once more of his weariness. 'She died three years ago,' he said quietly. 'Time heals all wounds. My grief was not for myself, but for her.' He moved his shoulders. 'It was a Muslim marriage.'

Realising at once that the cryptic remark

196

had a far greater significance than his manner suggested, Gena was about to ask him to explain. But he spoke first, and there was a new intensity in his gaze.

'And it was because you thought I was married that you refused to accept what was happening between us?' he demanded.

She nodded and looked down at her hands. 'Something happened to me . . . a long time ago . . .' It was difficult to talk about, though not because it still hurt. David was right, time was a great healer, and had it not been for that dreadful night she would not be here now. What made it difficult was the fact that she had never spoken of it before. There had been no one to tell, no one who cared, no one to whom she could turn for comfort and support. And she had been so ashamed, believing what he had told her: that it was her fault, that she had invited it, that it was all she was good for.

'He was married?' David supplied, and the mixture of anger and compassion in his voice caused sudden tears to blur her vision. She nodded, compressing her lips, unable to speak. 'And that was the *only* reason?'

The jagged edge to his voice, the new note of strain, told Gena her guess had been correct. He *had* assumed her rejection was due to his background.

Releasing some of her own tension in a deep sigh and taking her courage in both hands, she raised her eyes to his. Desperate to convince him, she stopped trying to hide her feelings and, for the first time, let him see the love that had changed her life. It softened her features, bathing them in a radiant glow and glistened in her tear-bright eyes. 'Oh, David,' her smile was tender, 'what other possible reason could there be?'

A multitude of expressions played across his face. 'Gena?' he whispered. And then she was in his arms, her body pressed to his, and he was holding her so tight that she could hardly breathe.

With unsteady fingers he smoothed her hair back from her face, his eyes devouring her as he murmured hoarse, incoherent words. He bent his head and his mouth found hers in a kiss that was both an act of homage and a surrender to passion, so long restrained. Their lips clung, hot and sweet, moving with a growing pressure as they sought to lose themselves in one another, all doubt and uncertainty swept away by a rising hunger that mere kisses could not assuage.

Gena could feel the thunder of David's heartbeat against her breast. His breathing was swift and ragged. One hand cupped her head while the other slid down her spine to mould her to him. Sweet fire surged through her lower body, heating her blood with a fever of urgency that made her moan softly.

Tearing his lips from hers, David rained tiny

kisses on her closed eyelids, her temple and cheekbone. But, as he sought her mouth once more, his chin scraped across her face and she yelped.

He drew back, brow furrowed, his dark eyes burning like twin coals. 'What is it? Did I hurt you?' The huskiness in his voice made her legs weak.

Gena grimaced, laughing breathlessly, her whole body tingling. 'It's your beard.'

David ran a hand quickly over his jaw and grinned at the rasping sound. 'Sorry,' he was rueful. 'Hell, of all the times to need a shave.'

Gena touched his cheek tenderly. 'Let's face it, neither of us expected this to happen.' She gazed up at him, drinking him in. 'I can hardly believe . . .' she whispered.

He caught her hand and kissed the palm, his lips warm and soft, the stubble abrasive, like coarse sandpaper. 'I will shower and shave.' His deep voice flowed over her like melted chocolate.

Gena made an effort to gather her wits. 'While you do that, I'll get a meal ready.'

He released her hand and stretched, flexing his broad shoulders. The movement reminded her that he had had little sleep since she left. 'You can leave that till I come out, if you like,' he offered.

Gena spread her hands. 'I've got to learn some time. I may as well start now.'

David's eyes gleamed with laughter as he

groaned. 'I was afraid of that.'

'Would you rather starve?' she retorted.

His face lit up. 'I have a choice?'

'No, you don't!' As she lunged at him, arm raised, David backed away towards the door leading to the shower.

'Just for tonight,' he grinned, 'do us both a favour. Use the tinned stuff.'

'You'll pay for that,' Gena warned, exhilaration making her heart sing.

'I'm counting on it,' he hissed and, raising one black brow in a look that sent her colour and temperature soaring, he closed the door behind him.

## CHAPTER NINE

David pushed his plate to one side and smiled across at Gena. 'That was delicious.'

'Honestly?' She blushed at her own eagerness and, lowering her eyes, caught sight of his plate and the small, congealing mound on it.

'Honestly,' he confirmed. 'The rice was very tender.'

'What you really mean,' Gena retorted drily, 'is that it was overcooked.' She sighed. 'And I was terrified it wouldn't be done enough. To tell you the truth, I had such a struggle getting that damn tin-opener to work, I forgot all about the rice.'

'How—er—what exactly went into the meat sauce?' David enquired.

'You didn't like it,' Gena said miserably.

'Yes, I did. I just said so. I simply wondered what you had found in the cupboard. We have to restock for the next team.'

Gena eyed him suspiciously, still convinced he was merely being kind. 'One tin of stewed steak, one of tomatoes and one of butter beans. I also added some boiled onions.

'Ah.' David nodded. 'Anything else?'

'I found a tub of dried herbs, so I put some of those in, for flavour.'

David's mouth flickered. 'How much did you put in?'

'Just what it said, a spoonful.'

'What size spoon?'

Gena stared at him, a small frown etching a furrow between her brows. 'I—well—there was a mark on the tub, I couldn't read—it wasn't very clear . . .' She faltered and caught her lip between her teeth.

'What size spoon?' he repeated, his eyes dancing with laughter.

She grimaced. 'A large one. I thought it tasted a bit strong.' She blew out a gusty sigh of self-contempt. 'One more culinary disaster to add to the list.'

'You exaggerate. Besides,' he pointed out, 'no one can be brilliant at everything. How many women do you know who can fly a helicopter?'

'I'm not belittling that,' Gena replied moodily. 'Lord knows, I worked hard enough to achieve it. But you could hardly say it was one of the basic necessities of everyday life. I don't feel like a normal woman at all.'

'And what, in your view, is a *normal* woman?' he demanded.

She could hear the undertone of amusement in his voice but was not angry or hurt, for she knew he was laughing with her, not at her. Yet she couldn't bring herself to respond. She felt too uncertain, too vulnerable. Resting her chin on her palms, Gena shrugged. 'You know what I mean. I'm the sort of person who invariably burns toast and lets the milk boil over. I can barely sew on a button and knitting is totally beyond me. My flat looks as though I'm just camping in it. Though I suppose,' she allowed, 'that's partly because I'm away such a lot.'

'The skills you mention, anyone can learn,' David was brusque. 'But intelligence, courage and compassion are inborn, and far more important. So is the capacity to love.' He raised his eyes, holding her gaze above the debris of the meal. Outside, the wind howled and whined, rattling the outer door.

Gena's breath caught in her throat. How handsome he was. Freshly shaved, his thick hair neatly combed and still damp from the shower, he now wore a pale blue shirt beneath

202

a navy sweater. The colour emphasised the bronze colour of his skin, and the whites of his onyx eyes. Even the shadows, like sooty thumbprints beneath his lower lashes, added something to his attractiveness, a hint of vulnerability in an otherwise invincible façade.

'Genuine caring is not dependent on domestic skills.' His deep voice was impatient. 'Of course they are useful, but when a spotless house and beautifully cooked food are a substitute for emotional closeness,' he looked away, 'a relationship becomes as arid as a desert.'

Reaching across the table, Gena touched his hand, stroking the strong fingers that played restlessly with a knife. Instinctively she sensed that his last remark related directly to his earlier cryptic statement.

'David?' she said softly. He glanced up. 'What you said, about your marriage being a Muslim one, what did you mean?'

Turning his hand over, he captured hers between both of his. He hesitated, but Gena realised it was not reluctance, only an attempt to order his thoughts which made him pause.

'I was twenty-six when I married,' he began, 'which in my country is late for a man. But I was still studying for my Ph.D. and because of that I had little time for a social life. No doubt you already know that Turkey is ninety-nine per cent Muslim, and in Muslim countries arranged marriages are the custom.' He smiled

203

at her. 'This does *not* mean that one day we are presented to a stranger and told, this is your bride, or groom. Nor do we have child-betrothals as they do in India.'

'So what does happen?' Gena was fascinated. There was still so much she had to learn about him.

'Well, in my case, my parents let it be known among their friends and acquaintances that I was contemplating marriage. Those with daughters of suitable age arranged a dinner party or dance to which my parents and I were invited so I could meet the girl and the two of us could decide if we wished to get to know one another better.' He stopped. 'What is it? You look . . . doubtful.'

Gena shook her head. 'It's just . . . I can see it has its points, but . . . isn't it all a bit cold-blooded? It reminds me of a cattle-market.'

'Mmm,' he murmured, his expression pensive. His dark eyes gleamed as one brow rose and he enquired in silken tones, 'Don't the English upper classes have a very similar system? I believe it's called "the season". The term always makes me think of hunting,' he added drily. 'I'm sure you must have heard of it. Parents organise coming-out balls to present their daughters in society, and there is a positive glut of dinners, dances, and supper-parties at which these young women hope to attract the attentions of prospective husbands.'

Involuntarily, Gena grinned. 'All right, all

right, point taken. The trouble with you is you know too much.'

His smile faded as he gazed into her eyes. 'Despite all my education and the countries I've visited, never before have I met anyone like you. But I believe now that was a good thing.'

Cold fingers clawed at Gena's stomach. 'Oh?' she croaked. 'Why do you say that?'

David's smile returned, softening the planes and angles into which exhaustion had drawn his strong features. 'Because until now I would not have understood or appreciated those qualities that make you the very special person you are. You have great loyalty.'

Gena's eyes flickered for an instant, knowing he referred to Jamie.

'But more than that, you have, I think, a deep well of love in you which has never been tapped.' His features tightened as he looked into the past. 'Some people have an ocean of love to give, others only a cupful. They cannot be blamed, it is just the way they are. Habiba, my wife, was such a person. I did not realise this until—' He fell silent for a moment, looking at Gena's hand held fast in his own.

'She was twenty-three, a college graduate, and worked as an infant teacher.' He glanced up at Gena, his mouth twisting briefly. 'It is only in rural villages that women still wear the veil and work in the fields with babies strapped to their backs. Anyway, her parents, and mine, were delighted when we decided, after our third meeting, to become engaged. The wedding took place six weeks later.'

Gena's eyes widened. 'That was quick.' Her free hand flew to her mouth as if to stop the words. 'Oh, David, I'm sorry. That was awfully rude—'

'No.' He shook his head, meeting her gaze head on. 'Gena, in the short time I've known you, you have rarely stopped to examine your words before speaking.' The smile that curved his mouth also lit up his eyes. As Gena coloured, he added softly, 'I would not wish it any other way.' He squeezed her hand. 'A Muslim marriage is based on practical considerations and not, as in the western world, on emotion. Similar backgrounds, social status and education mean less scope for misunderstanding and a greater chance of love growing. At least,' he added with an unconsciously wistful shrug, 'that's the theory. Habiba was a wonderful housewife. As well as her degree, she had all the skills you envy. She was also anxious to have children. I would have preferred a few years just for ourselves first. Since leaving home for university at eighteen I had lived alone. Sharing my life with someone was a new experience for me. I believed we both needed time to adjust.'

Gena was conscious of very mixed emotions as he talked. Jealousy tore with sharp talons at her fragile self-confidence as her imagination conjured up all too vivid images of David with this apparent paragon of Turkish virtue. And yet she didn't want him to stop. His life with Habiba was in the past, it was no threat to her. It was also an experience which, obviously, had affected him deeply, colouring his outlook and attitudes. To know him as she so desperately wanted to, Gena realised she had to accept, without reservation, all that had happened in his life. For that had made him the man he now was, the man she loved.

'But,' David continued, rubbing her knuckles with his thumb as he talked, 'she pleaded that even if she became pregnant quickly, we would still have many months before the child was born. It was clearly so important to her that I agreed. I was busy with my studies and I wanted her to be happy.' He paused. 'She conceived almost at once. She was radiantly happy and naturally our families were delighted.' His voice had an edge to it. 'The alliance was cemented, the succession assured. So I put my doubts aside. But she miscarried at four months.' His expression grew bleak. 'She lost six babies in five years, and each time it was as though a little part of her died too. Yet her determination to bear a child grew even stronger. She was desperate to prove to her family and mine that she was not a failure.'

Pity for the poor Turkish girl welled up in Gena. For all her education and modern ways,

Habiba had still been a prisoner of tradition.

'Fortunately,' David went on, 'her doctor managed to convince her that her body needed time to recover, and recommended that she wait two years before trying again.'

Gena noticed he said *she* and not *we*.

'By this time the marriage was under great strain. Still, I hoped that with all thoughts of children set aside for a while, we might somehow . . .' He shook his head. 'She did try, but it soon became clear that the reservations I had had at the beginning about her feelings for me were only too well-founded. I believe she loved me as much as she was capable of loving any man, but being a mother mattered more to Habiba than being my wife. I was merely the means to help her achieve that end.'

He fell silent, and Gena wondered if reliving the memories was proving too painful for him. But she *had* to know the rest. She sensed also that he needed to finish the story in order to finally free himself from certain chains that still bound him to the past.

'What happened?' she prompted quietly, laying her hand over his.

He hunched his massive shoulders. 'Towards the end of the two years we were arguing almost continuously. I was reluctant to put either of us through all that strain again, and I was genuinely concerned for her physical and emotional health. She went to stay with her mother for ten days. To be honest, I found it a relief to be alone. When she came back she was almost like the girl I had married—laughing, teasing, full of high spirits.' His mouth thinned. 'Anyway, inevitably we made love. And just as inevitably, she got pregnant.'

His voice altered, becoming thoughtful. 'This time it was different. There was a serenity about her, a new assurance. She even continued to show affection for me. The other times—' He made a brief dismissive gesture with one hand. But Gena sensed that behind it lay years of rejection, and her heart bled for him. 'I began to hope that perhaps we could actually build something worth while. We had both invested an enormous amount in the marriage and if, as it now appeared, Habiba had at last achieved her dearest wish, surely some of her happiness would spill over on to me.'

Gena blinked to clear the sudden mist of tears as compassion for David engulfed her. How lonely he must have been. The Turkish girl's behaviour was beyond her comprehension. To have a husband like David and see him not as a man, to adore and cherish and enjoy, but only as a potential father? How could she be so blind? Children were only a part of the marriage union, not the sole purpose. Children grew up, left home, married and had families of their own. If they had been a woman's whole reason for living, what would be left but silence and emptiness?

209

She gripped David's hands tightly. 'Go on,' she whispered.

'Half-way through the fourth month of her pregnancy, Habiba's doctor decided she should go into hospital. Apparently there is a minor operation which can help prevent miscarriage. In view of her history, it seemed a wise thing to do. I took her in at ten in the morning. She was due in theatre at two that afternoon and the nurse said I could pick her up the following morning.' He kept his gaze on their entwined hands.

'We said goodbye, and I wished her luck. She laughed and said she didn't need it, not this time.' His voice grew flat. 'Four and a half hours later she died. They told me she'd had a rare allergic reaction to the anaesthetic. No one's fault, quite unforeseeable, a tragic accident.'

He raised his head, his eyes diamond-hard. 'I grieved for her, for the waste of her life. But I was full of anger too. Marriage had not given either of us what we had sought.'

He stood up abruptly, his conflicting emotions clearly demanding the release of movement. Hands in his pockets, he stood at the larger window and looked out. Rain lashed against the glass, barely deflected by the metal grille.

Gena watched the tall figure. She could see his brooding reflection in the glass and ached for him. 'One thing life has taught me,' she said quietly, 'and it has been a painful lesson, is that there are no guarantees. We are programmed in childhood with other people's ideas of how things should be. So when our lives don't follow the set pattern, or we realise it's not what we want, we're at a loss. I had a rotten childhood, you had an unhappy marriage. It's tough, but no one promised life would be easy. What's past is gone. It's what we do *now* that counts.'

David remained unmoving for several long moments, then swung round, fixing her with his dark, penetrating gaze. 'And what,' he enquired in deep, velvet tones, 'would *you* suggest we do now?'

Caught off guard, Gena stared at him uncertainly, then she glimpsed the gleam in his eyes and the fleeting upward tilt of the corners of his mouth.

A thrill tingled through her, and her heart seemed to skip a beat. She thought of the long night stretching ahead of them and, for an instant, found it difficult to breathe. Shyness and nervous excitement mingled to set her pulses racing.

Laughter bubbled up inside her. 'There's only one answer to that,' she murmured softly. As he raised one black brow, his eyes narrowing fractionally, she indicated the table with a sweeping gesture. 'The dishes.'

'I'm not at all sure I approve of this sudden domestic urge of yours,' David grumbled as he poured boiling water into the washing-up bowl.

'Too bad,' Gena retorted drily. 'I am not facing this lot in the morning. That sauce will have dried to the consistency of concrete, and guess who will be too busy in the receiver-room to help? We both ate, we'll both wash up.'

David laughed out loud. 'My goodness, you're bossy. Anyone overhearing this conversation would think we'd lived together for years.'

Hot colour flooded Gena's face. She put the dirty dishes down on the draining board. 'I wouldn't know.' She cast him a shy, sidelong glance. 'I've never lived with anyone, I don't know the form.'

Swiftly wiping his hands on the drying cloth then tossing it on to the worktop, David grasped her shoulders and turned her towards him, tilting her chin with his index finger. His eyes searched hers, then he bent and, with exquisite gentleness, kissed her lips. 'I'm glad,' he murmured fiercely. Turning back to the sink, he plunged his hands into the bubble-topped water, needing, Gena sensed, to be busy. 'I know that is selfish of me, and I know I am guilty of double standards. But then, I am on occasion, as you say, an arrogant, chauvinistic bastard. All yesterday and last night I cursed myself for a fool. I believed I had lost you. I realise now I almost did, through my stiff-necked pride. You would not have come back but for Jamie. I am forever in his debt.' The flow of words faltered. 'A week ago I did not know you existed, but since we met . . .' his voice roughened, 'you have changed my life, Gena.'

She looked up at the strong profile, glimpsing behind it the uncertainty which kept his eyes averted, and joy fizzed like champagne in her blood. 'Oh, David,' she whispered, and rested her forehead against his shoulder. Who said dreams never came true? Surely he was telling her he loved her?

The howling wind reached a new level of ferocity and rain hit the window with a sound like gravel. Gena felt a stirring of unease and raised her head.

Outside the strain on the already weakened wire became too great. It snapped, whipping through the air and entangling itself in the framework of the slender metal pylon to which all the receiver antennae were attached.

Another violent squall hit and, with a scream of tortured metal, the aerial crumpled at the base and tipped sideways, its weight snapping two more wires as it fell on to the rocks.

Inside the cabin, David and Gena heard the tearing crash and froze.

'The helicopter.'

'The radio mast,' they mouthed in unison.

Gena would have bolted for the door had

David not grabbed her. 'There are two sets of oilskins in the store next to the generator-room,' he rapped. 'You fetch those while—'

'Hadn't we better see what's happened first?' She cut in anxiously.

'It has *already* happened, we can't change that,' he replied tersely. 'In this rain we'll be soaked to the skin in seconds. Whatever damage has been done will take time to put right, assuming repairs are even possible. Running around like headless chickens won't help. Now get the oilskins while I light the Tilley lamps, then at least we should be able to see what we are doing.'

Even with the sleeves and trouser bottoms rolled up, the waterproofs were far too big for Gena and her movements were clumsy and awkward as she followed David down the steps carrying one of the lamps. Despite the sou'wester tied under her chin, the rain, blown horizontally by storm-force gusts, lanced needle-sharp and ice-cold against her skin. Within moments her face and neck were streaming, and water trickled down the inside of her upturned collar to soak into her shirt and sweater.

But Gena was barely conscious of the discomfort, far more concerned with finding out what had caused the terrible crash. Grateful for its bright, steady light, she held the lamp high and picked her way as swiftly as she dared across the slippery ground. A gust caught her, like a giant fist in her back, and pushed her roughly forward. She slid and stumbled towards the helicopter, her heart in her mouth. *If it was damaged* . . .

'It's OK,' David shouted, his voice snatched and carried away by the howling wind. To make sure she understood, he pointed to the helicopter and gave her a thumbs-up, then turned to scramble up the rocks, his lamp swinging wildly.

Gena felt almost sick with relief. She gave the aircraft one last, careful scrutiny. The rotors, though flexing under the wind's pressure, were held securely by the sleeves and stays. She crouched beside the skids, holding the lamp so that its light fell on the shackles. They too were holding. Letting out a distinctly shaky sigh, Gena straightened up and, wiping the rain from her eyes, staggered towards the cliff-face which protected the rear of the cabin.

She could see David's lamp. He was coming *down*. 'What is it?' she yelled.

'Trouble.' He jumped the last few feet, landing beside her, grim-faced and out of breath.

'Bad?' She blinked the rainwater away, and shook her head, but the deluge just went on.

'The worst. The radio mast is down. The recorders won't be receiving any signals from the out-stations. Without that information, the whole project is in jeopardy.'

'What do we have to do to get the mast back

up?' Gena's teeth were chattering. Already her face was stiff with cold and she was having difficulty shaping words.

David's eyes gleamed like a cat's in the lamplight as he glowered down at her. Rainwater glistened on his face and dripped from his nose and chin. 'You go back inside,' he ordered. 'You're frozen already.'

'Don't be ridiculous,' Gena yelled back immediately. 'You can't possibly do it alone. We're supposed to be a team. I may be a dead loss with a saucepan, but I know how to use a spanner.'

They glared at one another a moment longer, then David let out an explosive growl. 'You are the most obstinate—'

'You're wasting valuable time,' Gena interrupted.

'*All right.* But if you—'

'What do we need?' she cut across him again, holding herself rigid against the spasms of shivering that racked her, forcing her to clench her teeth.

'Heavy-gauge wire for new stays, rope and pulley to rig up a winch—' David rattled off a list of items as they made their way over the treacherous ground towards the back entrance and the store-room. The water running down the cliff-face had formed deep puddles and Gena could feel the icy chill of the water strike through her fleece-lined boots.

It took four hours to get the mast back in

place. Four hours of knifing wind and driving rain. Four hours during which Gena scrambled awkwardly about fetching tools, or crouched in muscle-cramped misery high on the exposed rocks, hauling on ropes and wires.

By the time they had finished, Gena's hands were literally blue with cold and so numb that she could no longer grip the spanner holding the shackles on the new stay wires while David tightened the bolts and screws.

Despite the protective oil-skins, she was soaked through and chilled to the bone, her face set in a grimace of agony.

Back in the store-room, David helped her out of the wet-weather gear, hanging it on nails to drip dry. He stripped off his own, then hustled her in through the back door, but instead of going straight to the kitchen he steered her left into the bathroom. There was barely room for the two of them.

'Get undressed,' he ordered, leaning into the cubicle and switching on the hot water. Steaming spray gushed from the shower head. 'I should never have let you talk me into—'

'Stop nagging,' Gena broke in, her teeth chattering violently as she tried to force her dead fingers to grip the lower edge of her sweater so she could pull it off. 'It's done now, and if it weren't for me you'd still be out there. So stop grumbling and be grateful for a change. Better still, go and put the kettle on.' Now she was out of the chilling wind and rain, the circulation was beginning to return to her hands and feet, and it hurt.

'Will you be all right?' David's voice was raw-edged with concern, and Gena realised she must look even worse than she felt.

She nodded, biting her lip against the red-hot needles of pain stabbing her hands and feet, and managed to fight free of her sweater.

'I'll go and put hot-water bottles in your bed. Sure you'll be OK?'

She nodded again, keeping her head down so he wouldn't see the pain etched on her face. It was no good being a heroine outside and collapsing the moment she came back in. But her fingers felt like overstuffed sausages. They still wouldn't work properly and even touching anything was torture.

David disappeared and Gena struggled with the buttons on her shirt, but her hands were so weak she just couldn't get hold of them. Her eyes filled with tears of fury and frustration and she slumped against the wall.

David's head came round the door. 'Why aren't you in the shower?' he demanded.

'I can't undo my bloody shirt,' she sobbed.

Muttering in Turkish under his breath, his tone full of barely controlled anger, his hands infinitely gentle, within seconds David had stripped her of shirt, bra and panties and gently pushed her white, goose-pimpled body under the steaming spray.

Gena gave a shuddering sigh of relief and

closed her eyes. She had no idea how long she stood there. The pain in her hands and feet gradually receded and a delicious warmth and languor pervaded her body.

It was only as all her muscles relaxed that she realised how much energy she had used up holding her body tense against the cold.

Abruptly, the curtain rattled back, the water was switched off and she was enfolded in a soft, warm towel. Then two strong arms drew her out into the tiny steam-filled room and with brisk, impersonal thoroughness rubbed her dry.

With enormous difficulty, Gena dragged her eyes open and squinted up at David. His hair was tousled where he had rubbed it with a towel, and he was wearing his pyjama bottoms and a sweater. 'I c'n manage.' Exhaustion slurred her words, making her sound mildly drunk, and her movements as she attempted to push him away lacked co-ordination.

'Of course you can,' he soothed. 'I just don't want you to get cold again.' Hanging the towel over the rail, he dropped her nightshirt over her head, then helped her into her dressing-gown.

'I'm not helpless, you know,' Gena insisted, fighting to keep her eyes open. 'I'm not a baby.'

'No,' his tone was dry, 'indeed you aren't.' With his arm around her shoulders, he guided her through the kitchen and into the bedroom.

219

'In you get. Mind the bottles, they might be a bit hot.'

'Ohhhh.' Gena breathed a voluptuous sigh as she leaned back against the propped pillows and David drew the covers up over her. 'Oh, that's *gorgeous.*'

'Here,' David took a steaming mug of malted milk from the top of the chest of drawers and placed it in her hands, 'drink it all. I'll be back later.'

'Where are you going?' With the detachment that came from total physical exhaustion, Gena heard the note of fretfulness in her question.

'To check that the signals are coming in and that all the equipment is functioning properly. I won't be long.'

'You will come back?'

'Where else would I go?' he retorted gently. 'Now drink up.'

Gena had just swallowed the last drop when he returned. 'Is everything all right?' she asked, the anxiety in her weary voice at odds with her heavy-lidded slow blink.

David took the mug, set it back on the chest, and sat down on the bed beside her, taking her hand. 'Every-thing is fine. But it wouldn't have been if not for you. I am grateful, Gena. I couldn't have done it alone.'

'True,' she agreed, yawning, and grinned impishly. 'That's quite a debt. How will you ever repay me?'

He looked startled for a moment, then his eyes began to gleam. 'I shall have to give it some serious thought. Meanwhile, I think we'd both better get some sleep.'

Gena tightened her grip on his hand. 'David,' she could feel warm colour flooding her face, 'don't go. Stay with me.' She heard the plea as if it were someone else speaking and beyond her control. 'I—I just want to be close. I really believed I'd never see you again. So much has happened. I—' She shook her head, unable to go on.

Gently, he freed his hand and in one lithe movement pulled his sweater off, tossing it on to his bed. Still silent, he helped her out of her dressing-gown, then climbed in beside her and lay down on his back, drawing the covers over them both. Sliding his arm around her shoulders, he drew her to him and kissed her forehead. Tentatively, Gena reached for his mouth, but he laid his index finger on her lips. 'Go to sleep,' he whispered. 'Goodnight, Gena.'

Sighing with contentment, her eyes already closed, she snuggled against him, her head on his shoulder, one hand resting on his chest, the thick, silky hair curling around her fingers. She absorbed the warmth of his body like a sponge. For the first time in her life she felt utterly safe. 'I love you, David,' she murmured, already sliding into a deep, dreamless sleep.

Many hours later she stirred, climbing

towards consciousness as her hand encountered the smooth, warm skin of a naked back. Her touch was met with a soft grunt, and in the twilight world between sleeping and waking Gena smiled and curled her body around David's, resting her arm along the cotton-covered curve of his hip and down the long length of hard-muscled thigh.

On the edge of her consciousness she was aware of him stirring. Then he turned towards her and, sliding his arm beneath her, drew her against him. Their bodies, warm and relaxed from sleep, met, and Gena revelled in the sensation.

With a soft sound deep in his throat, David's arm tightened around her and he ran his upper hand down her spine from shoulder to hip, moulding her to him.

She was immediately aware of his arousal and a leaping tongue of flame erupted from the centre of her body and sent liquid heat coursing through her veins.

He groaned, and the next instant his mouth was on hers, hungry, demanding, and Gena clung to him, buffeted by a powerful urgency that swept her up like a leaf in a gale. It was a feeling she had never experienced before. It frightened and exhilarated, making her whimper and gasp as her heart raced and excitement tightened like a watchspring deep inside her.

Then, without warning, he pushed her away,

wrenching her arms from his neck and tearing his lips from hers as he rolled out of bed.

Gena's eyes flew wide with shock at the brutal haste of his withdrawal. She murmured incoherently, still dazed by his passionate embrace and the thrilling response he had aroused in her.

David stood at the window, head bent, his arms high, palms flat against the wall. His powerful body was silhouetted against the lemon and primrose dawn. Gena could see his ribcage heaving as he sucked in deep breaths.

'David?' she ventured softly, her voice cracked and husky.

'Go back to sleep,' he grated.

She raised herself on one elbow, concern clouding her face. Her whole body ached with an unfamiliar tension, an urgent hunger that craved the release only he could provide. 'Is something wrong?' Her mouth was swollen and throbbed from the pressure of his kisses. 'Aren't you feeling well?'

'I'm fine,' he said through gritted teeth. Pushing himself away from the window, the movement so sudden that it made Gena flinch, he snatched up his sweater from the bed and, striding to the chest, dragged open a drawer and took out fresh clothes. He slammed the drawer shut and glanced at her over his shoulder. 'Please,' it was half plea, half command, the tone hoarse and tightly controlled, 'it's early yet. Go back to sleep.' He added under his breath, 'This is going to be one hell of a long day.'

## CHAPTER TEN

Gena lay down again on her side, curling herself into a ball. She pulled the bedclothes up to her neck and burrowed into the pillow, desperately seeking warmth and comfort.

*Why* had he left her so suddenly? He had wanted her, of that there was no doubt. And surely he must have realised she felt the same? Unless—David's background, his mixed heritage, had blended in him the sophistication of the west with the eastern concept of honour. Did he feel that making love to her signified a commitment on his part? A commitment he was not yet ready for, or perhaps did not want?

No, that could not be true. He had told her how glad he was that she had come back, *that he needed her.* But for what?

Had there been yet another misunderstanding? She had believed he meant that he needed her emotionally, as a woman. Could he, in fact, have meant he needed her professional skills, as a colleague, and for company, to ease the pressures on him? For David Halman even that would have been a tough admission to make.

Yes, he was considerate and thoughtful, and

had been genuinely concerned about her getting so cold and wet. He made no secret of the fact that she was unlike any other woman he had known and that this attracted him to her. And he had kissed her with a passion that set her on fire, sending shivers of delight along every nerve and turning her legs to jelly.

But he had said nothing of the future, made no reference to what would happen *after* they left here.

Could it be he did not see a future together for them? That his admiration and respect, and the attraction she held for him, were confined only to the time they were here at the base? And that after the quake they would go their separate ways?

Restlessly, Gena turned on her back and stared at the ceiling. A dull ache nagged in the pit of her stomach. He had never said he loved her. Yes, he found her sexually exciting, but that could be due as much to the fact that he was a strong, healthy, virile man who had been a widower for three years as to whatever physical or emotional appeal she possessed.

Self-doubt engulfed her like a breaking wave, its undertow sucking her down into black despair. She loved him. But he did not love her, so, being an honourable man, despite his desire, the opportunity, and her willing eagerness, he had backed off. That it had cost him dearly had been only too clear. But that only confirmed her deduction.

While she had fallen head over heels, entranced by this man who matched her in every way, who challenged her mind, her body and her emotions, he had seen their relationship only as an interlude. Ahslan was a place out of time. While they were here, alone, it was as if the rest of the world had ceased to exist. *But it hadn't.* Life went on just the same. While she had succumbed to the illusion, David had remained firmly in touch with reality.

A door slammed, making her start violently. Sleep was out of the question. Gena sat up and hugged her knees. She loved him and she had told him so. How was she to face him now? How should she behave? Offhand and careless? Hiding all the hurt and yearning behind a barrier of wisecracks and work, making jobs to do if she had to?

She rested her forehead on her knees. He'd see through it in an instant, and his sympathy was more than she could bear. But nor would she play the tragedy queen. He had not asked her to fall in love with him. The problem she now faced was not his fault. It had simply happened and, regardless of the outcome, she could not regret it. She had learned an enormous amount through having known him and was, she truly believed, a nicer person. That was what she would cling to. That thought, and her dignity. Loving someone was nothing to be ashamed of. It was how one

226

handled the situation when the gift was returned, unwanted, that mattered.

Gena raised her head and sucked in a long, slow breath, drawing on her inner reserves, steeling herself. She would take her lead and example from David. As he had said, it was going to be a very long day.

She dressed quickly in a clean shirt of cream brushed cotton, fawn cords, and her coral sweater, then ran a comb through her hair and, stiffening her spine, opened the door.

'Gena?' David called from the alcove.

She paused, tense, still holding the door-handle, and forced herself to relax. 'Yes?'

'I'm just making fresh coffee. Is that all right, or would you prefer something else?'

Acutely sensitive to nuance, she heard the underlying strain in his voice. He had to be finding this every bit as difficult as she was, though obviously for different reasons. 'Coffee will be fine, thanks,' she called. 'I'll be back in a moment.'

Splashing water on to her face to rinse away the soap, Gena thought she detected an odd smell. But it was so fleeting, she shrugged it off.

She ran the tap to wet her toothbrush, and wrinkled her nose at the faint sulphurous whiff of rotten eggs. The minty foam freshened her mouth, but as she rinsed and spat, she noticed the water had a strange bitter taste.

As she returned to the kitchen, David was

putting the coffee-pot on the table. He glanced up and quickly looked away again.

Gena swallowed. 'Is it my imagination, or does the water taste peculiar?'

This time he didn't look away. 'You noticed it? I wondered if it was just me.' His mouth widened in a brief, self-mocking grin that pierced Gena like a dart.

*She had to get a grip on herself.* He had praised her courage. She'd better start showing some.

'What do you call it,' he snapped his fingers as he sought the phrase he wanted, 'wishful thinking?'

Gena showed her puzzlement. 'Sorry, I don't understand.'

David shook his head and sat down on the stool opposite. 'It is I who should apologise.' He kept his gaze on the coffee as he poured. 'I didn't explain. Sometimes before a seismic event, certain phenomena occur. Wells and springs alter their levels, the water can become cloudy or discoloured. Sometimes it has an unusual smell and a strong taste.'

'What causes it?' Gena asked.

'We are not absolutely certain, but the most likely theory is the release of underground gases as the rock begins to fracture.'

Gena cupped her hands around the mug David had just filled and pushed towards her. 'H-how long before the quake do these things happen?'

David shrugged and shook his head. 'It varies. It could be days, even weeks. Then again, it may only be hours.'

Abruptly, Gena raised the mug to her lips and sipped the strong, sweet liquid, barely tasting it as she fought to keep her mouth steady.

*Only hours.* After the quake, David would collect up all the data and they would leave. She would fly him to Ankara and it would all be over.

Suddenly remembering, she caught her breath, putting down her mug so quickly some of the coffee spilled. 'Th-those people—in the mountains—'

'I set the flares off as soon as I got up,' he reassured her. 'The chances are they will have already seen the other signs and be moving out, anyway. But just to be certain I've radioed Van airport and asked that they relay any information as soon as they receive it.'

'What other signs?' Despite the hot coffee, Gena's throat was uncomfortably dry.

'Animals know when earthquakes are coming long before our instruments pick up any change in the signals,' he explained, his gaze focused on the mug in front of him. He radiated tension, and Gena's stretched nerves tightened even further. 'They become restless and agitated. The herdsmen know their animals well and recognise unusual behaviour at once.'

'But will they recognise the reason for it?' Gena pressed.

David nodded. 'Of course. Tremors and quakes happen frequently in this part of Turkey. The seismic gap which brought me out here covers only a relatively small area.'

'The animals,' Gena persisted, reluctant, already forseeing the answer she dreaded, yet knowing she could not hide from the truth, 'they would not exhibit this behaviour *weeks* in advance, would they?'

Head bent, David was turning his mug round and round in jerky circles. Pushing it away, he stood up. 'No,' he admitted bluntly. 'I—I must go and check the recorders. There were a number of microshocks during the night.' *Indeed there were.* Gena bit her lip. 'Please,' he urged, 'you should eat something.'

A buzzing sound reached them, making Gena jump. She had to get a grip on her nerves. At this rate she would be a gibbering wreck by the evening.

'It's only the radio,' David assured her, and she felt even worse that he had noticed. 'I expect it will be the report on tribe movements I asked for. Excuse me.'

'Of course.' Gena's knuckles were white. The politeness and formality were making her want to scream. He was right, she should eat, but the thought of food revolted her. Tension had contracted her stomach into a small tight knot.

She had to keep busy. It was the only way she could think of to disperse the anxiety and stress building up inside her like a pressure cooker.

'Oh, David,' she whispered, her eyes hot, tears pricking.

Quickly Gena stood up. Straightening her back, she gritted her teeth and began clearing the table.

When she had dried the dishes and made her bed, she washed and rinsed the sodden clothes David had left piled on the worktop. After wringing as much water from them as she could, her wrists aching from the effort, Gena carried them outside and hung them on her makeshift washing-line.

The ground was still wet and muddy, but the wind had died away completely. There was a strange stillness in the air, as though the day was holding its breath, waiting. Even the muffled sound of the generator's engine seemed unnaturally loud.

A shiver feathered down Gena's spine like a single drop of icy water. Even as she chided herself for being fanciful and over-dramatic, unease pervaded the atmosphere like an invisible mist, and she knew it did not all come from within herself.

She turned from hanging David's sweater over the guard rail edging the steps up to the cabin door, and surveyed the valley, absently rubbing her upper arms. She wasn't cold, and yet . . .

There wasn't a single sign of life. No birds spiralled in the pale sky. No animals scuttled among the tumbled, barren rocks. There wasn't even a single blade of grass or wild flower.

There was a curiously leaden tinge to the sunshine. Gena shaded her eyes and squinted up at the sky. Turning slowly from east to west, her gaze reached the Musgüney mountains. Suspended just above a snow-capped ridge was the moon. It was full and seemed unnaturally large, as though much closer than usual. But it wasn't the magnified size which caused Gena's sharp intake of breath. Instead of the rich yellow-gold of harvest time, or the milky whiteness that silvered the water on a winter's night, the moon was dark, a sullen, brooding coppery-bronze.

Gena felt a sharp stab of real fear and immediately, automatically tried to rationalise it away. It was simply the result of unusual atmospheric conditions, a physical phenomenon with a simple explanation.

But her heart still pounded uncomfortably and the feeling of threat persisted. Steeling herself not to run, Gena walked with deliberate, measured tread back into the cabin.

Once more inside, her knuckles gleaming white as she gripped the edge of the sink and gulped in deep breaths, she was overcome with embarrassment. What on earth was happening to her? She was an intelligent, level-headed person, not normally given to ridiculous flights of fancy. Stress over the uncertainty of her relationship with David was beginning to affect her mental and emotional balance.

As the door opened, she flinched, covering her reaction by reaching for the kettle.

'I was right,' David said, closing the kitchen door behind him, filling the small room with his presence. He rubbed his hands together, the gesture betraying the strain gnawing at him.

'Aren't you always?' she quipped, striving for lightness, achieving a brittle artificiality which only emphasised the tension vibrating between them.

'The tribe should be well clear of the danger area by this evening,' he continued as if she hadn't spoken.

'Thank heaven for that,' Gena muttered in genuine and heartfelt relief. She glanced up, about to tell him about the moon and the eerie stillness, only to meet his eyes fixed on her with glittering intensity.

Her heart gave a sickening lurch and hammered against her ribs. All her resolutions splintered into fragments. *She loved him.* She had to hear the truth of his feelings, or lack of them, for her from his own lips. Better that, no matter how devastating, than this terrible seesawing between hope and despair.

'David?' she began, her throat painfully stiff, but he waved her to silence and turned to look out of the window, his whole body tensed, listening.

She froze, responding both to his action and her own barely controlled nervousness. *What now?*

'It's the army chopper,' he announced curtly, 'they're bringing the supplies. Can you move the Jet Ranger while they make the drop? There might be enough room, but—'

'Yes, of course,' Gena didn't wait for him to finish. She could have screamed with frustration, but almost at once it was smothered by dull hopelessness. Grabbing her jacket from the back of the door, she checked she had her keys and, as David went in to radio the army pilot and ask him to stand away while she took off, she hurried out to the Jet Ranger.

Why was she still fighting? What was the point? If there was no chance of a future with David, what difference did it make whether the conclusion came from his lips or her own reasoning? The result was the same.

She flew down the valley, trying *not* to think. She knew she could not take much more. Her nerves were almost at breaking-point. Soon, very soon, something would have to give.

The familiar actions of flying gradually soothed her, giving her the respite she so desperately needed. When she returned to the base an hour later, David was rolling the last of the fuel drums towards the store.

By the time she walked into the kitchen, David was already in the alcove, unpacking the boxes of fresh and tinned groceries and putting them away.

She hung up her jacket and, tugging her sweater down over her hips, touched her hair with a nervous movement, and started forward. 'Is there anything you'd like me to do?'

He jerked round, and from his startled expression she realised he had been so immersed in his own thoughts that he had not heard her come in.

They stared at one another. A tiny muscle flickered below his left eye as a variety of expressions chased fleetingly across his face, mirroring the conflict raging within him, and the battlefield of her own emotions.

She waited, holding herself rigid against the agony to come when he told her, as she knew he must, that he was sorry, there had obviously been a terrible misunderstanding.

'Gena?' His voice sounded as though it was being torn from his throat. 'I—I—will you answer me honestly if I ask you a question?'

She had to swallow before she could speak.

She stopped. She had been about to say that she had never lied to him. But that wasn't true. She *had* lied. The morning after they had met she had made every effort to convince him that his arrival in her life was of no consequence whatsoever. And she had gone on, not exactly *lying*, but trying to pretend, until the bitter-sweet truth had overwhelmed her and she had had no choice but to face the fact that she had fallen in love with him.

Clearing her throat, she lifted her chin. 'Yes, I will give you an honest answer.' After all, what did she have left to lose?

'Have you ever considered giving up your career?'

Gena was startled. She hadn't known what to expect, but still his question took her by surprise. His eyes bored into hers, but gave no clue to the thoughts behind them.

'No,' she answered.

He nodded imperceptibly. It was obviously the answer he had expected.

'Can you envisage a time or situation when you might do so?'

Gena frowned as she thought carefully. 'Only one,' she replied after a long pause.'

'And that is?'

She swallowed again, her throat curiously dry. 'If I ever had children.' She approached the sink. 'Excuse me, may I have a drink of water?'

'Of course.' He filled a mug and passed it to her. As their fingers touched briefly, so their eyes met.

'Do you plan to do so?'

'Have children? As I am not married, the

question does not arise.' She swallowed more water, clasping the mug tightly.

'But do you *want* them?'

She hesitated. His gaze sharpened, holding hers, daring her to break the contact. The tension between them vibrated like a taut wire. 'I—I've never really thought about it,' she replied slowly. 'Until now.'

*I want your child,* she thought. A son, with black hair and flashing eyes, and maybe a daughter too, who would have the gentle, thoughtful side of your nature. But not yet, perhaps not for several years. I would want you all to myself for a long time first.

Shaken by the vivid clarity of her thoughts, she raised an unsteady hand to her lips, aghast. Had she spoken aloud?

'And now?' he persisted, his deep voice urgent. 'Now you *have* thought about it?'

Gena was becoming agitated. 'What is the point of all this?' she demanded uncertainly. 'You said one question. This is an inquisition.'

'Please,' his voice was low, harsh, 'trust me.'

Placing the mug carefully on the draining-board, Gena turned her back and leaned against the sink, hugging her arms across her chest. David did not move. He stood barely a foot from her left shoulder, and even with her eyes closed Gena could feel his presence. Trust me, he said. What choice did she have? There was obviously a purpose behind this interrogation, and her replies were clearly of tremendous importance to him. But were they the right ones? She had no way of knowing, for his expression gave nothing away. All she could do was tell the truth and pray that what she said was what he wanted to hear.

Her fingers bit into her upper arms through the thickness of her sweater. 'Married to a man I loved,' she replied with exquisite care, 'yes, eventually I would want his children. But probably not for some time.'

The intensity faded from David's eyes and they glowed with a gentle warmth. 'Why wait?' he enquired softly.

'Because I'm selfish,' she retorted. 'I would want him all to myself for a while.' She shrugged. 'My ideas of marriage do not include immediately filling the house with other people.'

One corner of David's mouth twitched in a quick smile. 'So you wouldn't want hordes of relations, in-laws and so on, popping in and out?'

Gena felt a stirring of excitement deep inside her and tried, unsuccessfully, to smother it. 'It would be *lovely* to have friends and relations visit, but not too often, by invitation only, and for a limited time.'

David exploded into laughter. 'You're a hard woman.'

Gena shook her head. 'No,' she said calmly. 'It's a matter of priorities. The way I see it, if both partners in a marriage have a career, which is often the case now, then their time together is precious.'

The broad smile that revealed David's strong teeth was reflected in his eyes. He looked suddenly five years younger.

Gena felt as though she was balanced on a tightrope with soaring hope on one side and agonised fear that she could be wrong on the other.

David lifted his left hand and cupped the back of her head. His touch and the intimacy of the gesture acted on her like an electric shock. Every nerve vibrated, tingles ran down her spine and sudden heat flooded her body.

Turning her towards him, David looked deep into her eyes, his smile so full of tenderness her heart felt as though it would burst. '*Now* do you understand,' he demanded softly, 'why I would not make love to you this morning?'

Gena stared at him blankly. Then, like the sun emerging from behind a cloud, realisation dawned, and everything became clear. 'Ohhh,' she gasped, 'it never occurred to me—oh, what a *fool*—I thought—' She shook her head, blushing a deep rose.

'What did you think?' he asked gently. 'Tell me.' He cupped her face. His hands were warm.

Gena moved her shoulders in a gesture of acute embarrassment. 'I—I th-thought you felt that if we . . . it would be a sort of commitment, and you didn't want that.'

'Oh, my love,' David murmured, drawing her to him, his arms enfolding her, his cheek resting on her hair. 'I want you so much, it's tearing me apart. Leaving you this morning was the hardest thing I've ever done, but I had no choice. I have already made one terrible mistake in my life. We have known each other only a short time and neither of us, I think, expected this to happen.'

Gena slid her arms around his waist, revelling in the closeness of his powerful body, and nestled her head in the curve between his neck and shoulder. 'You can say that again,' she whispered.

David's arms tightened. 'After this morning, waking beside you, feeling you so warm and responsive, *so giving* after all you had been through yesterday, I knew for certain you are the woman I want to share the rest of my life with. We have much still to learn about each other and this will take, I think, a lifetime. But some things must be resolved *before* marriage; if not, they will destroy. You understand?'

Gena nodded against his shoulder. 'That was the reason for all those questions?'

He hugged her. 'Do you forgive me?'

She kissed the warm brown skin of his throat, in-haling the scent of him, *her man.* 'There is nothing to for—' She broke off, momentarily giddy. She clutched at David, stiffening in his arms. 'My feet,' she muttered,

240

'it's like pins and needles, but'

The sensation grew stronger, becoming a definite vibration that travelled up her legs and through her body, making her teeth chatter. At the same time she heard a low rumble. It was similar to the growl of distant thunder, but had a booming resonance unlike any storm she had ever known.

David grabbed her shoulders, setting her apart from him, his face taut with excitement. *'This is it!'* As he spoke, alarm bells started ringing in the receiver-room, adding their strident clamour to the deep, grinding reverberation, and Gena realised she was experiencing her first earthquake.

The whole cabin was vibrating. Crockery and tinned food rattled, the furniture all shifted slightly. The floor undulated beneath Gena's feet and an instant's pure terror dewed her with cold perspiration as she recalled his words. 'You can't run away from an earthquake.' Closing her eyes tight, she clung to him.

The noise gradually faded and the cabin stopped shaking. Gena didn't. The entire event had lasted less than a minute. Hunched against the din, Gena let go of David, and pressed her hands over her ears to shut out the insistent jangle of the bells.

Cupping her face, David kissed her gently but quickly, and giving her shoulders a quick, reassuring squeeze, he strode to the door and out into the receiver-room. A moment later the bells stopped. The silence was deafening.

Slowly, Gena lowered her hands and straightened up, letting her breath out in a long, shaky sigh. She felt decidedly light-headed. David reappeared, grinning widely. 'D-did you c-capture it?' she stuttered, her eagerness genuine, despite the shock.

He nodded. 'On the paper rolls the pen nearly shot off the graph. We'll get a more detailed analysis of distance, depth and magnitude from the tape-recordings once the signals are decoded and fed through a computer.' He put his arm around her shoulders and frowned at her continued trembling. 'My love, are you all right?'

She flashed him an unsteady grin. 'I will be, in a minute,' she stuttered, her teeth chattering violently in the aftermath of so much emotional upheaval. 'I g-guess this brings a whole new meaning to the phrase, *"the earth moved for them"*.'

David held her head between cherishing hands, his eyes dark pools brimming with adoration. 'I love you, Gena,' he said with soft intensity. 'I am proud to love you, and to ask you to be my wife. All I have is yours.'

It was too much for Gena. Tears welled up, hovered diamond-bright on her thick lashes, and spilled over to trickle down her pale cheeks. 'Oh, David, my dearest, I—'

'You *will* marry me?' he demanded, his

smile fading.

'Oh, *yes,*' Gena hiccuped as laughter stifled a sob. 'Of course I will.'

'When?' he rapped.

'As soon as you like.' She lifted her arms and slid them around his neck, glorying in the thickness of his black hair, and the powerful strength of his body as he held her close. The banked-down embers of desire flared into bright flame, and Gena whispered against his mouth. 'Please make it soon, David.'

He groaned, and muttered harshly, 'Do you think I need persuading? By the time we leave here tomorrow I will have used up a lifetime's will-power.' Deliberately he loosened his hold. 'Woman, show a little pity and put the bloody kettle on.'

Catching her lower lip between her teeth in an effort to conceal her smile of delight, Gena turned on the tap. 'We're leaving tomorrow?' she asked over her shoulder.

Leaning against the cupboard, his arms folded, David nodded. 'I want to get the tapes to the Earthquake Research Institute at Bogazici University as soon as possible.'

'But what about all the instruments? You know, the out-stations down the valley?'

'They stay. There's another team coming out in about ten days who will want the equipment. Where would you like to be married?'

Gena reached into the wall cupboard for

243

coffee and sugar. 'Why not here, in Turkey? This is your country.'

He gazed at her, his expression thoughtful. 'You are sure about that?' When she nodded decisively, he added, 'Is there anyone you would like to invite from England?'

Gena thought briefly of her father, then of Jamie and Helen, and shook her head. 'No. What about you? Who are you going to invite? You have a large family.'

'No one,' he said simply. 'My family attended my marriage to Habiba, they have had their celebration. This wedding is for you and me alone.'

Gena raised a radiant face to his. 'I'm so glad you feel that way. I mean, I'm looking forward to meeting them, and I hope they can accept me . . .'

'They will,' David said quietly. 'But it wouldn't make the slightest difference to me if they didn't. You are marrying me, not my family, and my loyalty is and always will be to you, my Gena, no one else.'

She flung herself at him, wrapping her arms around his neck, hugging him with all her strength. For the first time in her life she was truly loved. Wherever David was would be her home.

He rocked her gently to and fro. 'For our honeymoon I will show you the other faces of Turkey. We could go to the Mediterranean or Aegean coasts, they have a very special beauty.

It is said Mark Antony gave part of Turkey's southern shore to Cleopatra as a wedding gift. Translucent water laps endless beaches of white sand, and orange groves, banana plantations and pine forest line the shores. Or, if you like, we could go first to the Black Sea Coast where I was born. My father owns a tea plantation near the town of Rize. People born on this coast have a reputation for being very independent,' he added, his eyes gleaming.

'I'd never have guessed,' Gena retorted drily, then giggled as he bit her ear in retaliation. 'Tell me what it's like there, David.' She snuggled against him.

'Above the towns and fishing villages there are cherry orchards, hazelnut groves and tobacco plantations, and where the land is uncultivated masses of purple rhododendrons grow wild. Behind the hills, the Black Sea mountains rise almost vertically in places. They are covered in dense forest, but here and there, built into an almost sheer cliff face, you can see ancient monasteries.'

'How can I choose?' Gena sighed, glowing with happiness. 'It all sounds so beautiful, I want to see everything. There's only one difficulty—'

'If you are going to mention the cost,' David broke in, 'don't. I promise you, Gena, money is no problem.'

'No, it wasn't that. I mean, please don't think I'm not grateful—'

'Tell me what's on your mind,' he prompted gently.

'Well, do you think it will be very difficult for me to get a job here? I really do want to go on flying,' she blushed as he cocked one eyebrow, 'for a while, at—

'I'll make some enquiries,' he said. 'I know my father and his colleagues regularly use helicopters to go to Istanbul and Ankara for important meetings. There is a problem, however.' Gena looked quickly up at him. Catching his serious expression and slight frown, she missed the laughter dancing in his eyes. 'I had hoped you would want to spend the first year of our married life with me.'

Gena's eyes widened. 'But I do,' she protested. 'Of course I do. That's why I was asking about work.'

'Darling,' he said patiently. 'I won't be working in Turkey for at least another twelve months.'

Gena gaped at him. '*What?* Then where—'

'Scotland,' he replied, grinning broadly. 'Edinburgh, to be exact. This project, the reason I am here at Ahslan, is under the direction of the Global Seismology Research Group, based at BGS in Edinburgh. I shall be taking copies of all the data back there for detailed study.'

'*Oh!*' Gena gasped, momentarily speechless.

'As far as *your* job is concerned, and your new status as my wife, I'm sure that together we'll be able to work something out with your father.' He smiled at her, but beneath the velvet tones of his deep voice she had heard the hint of steel, and knew that never again would she have to fight alone. From now on David would be at her side, to protect and encourage her as husband, lover, friend and champion.

Gazing up at him, radiant, she touched his face with gentle fingers, her heart filled with awe, pride and overwhelming love. 'With you,' she vowed, 'I'll reach the stars.'